MAY STUART

PAUL C.R. MONK

A BLOOMTREE PRESS Book.

First published in 2019 by BLOOMTREE PRESS.

ISBN 978-1-9164859-4-5

Copyright © Paul C.R. Monk 2019

www.paulcrmonk.com

Formatting by Polgarus Studio.

Cover design by Books Covered.

BY THE SAME AUTHOR

In The Huguenot Chronicles trilogy:

Merchants of Virtue

Voyage of Malice

Land of Hope

Other works:

Strange Metamorphosis

Subterranean Peril

ONE

ON THE DAY when news of the English declaration of war against France reached Port-de-Paix, Captain Joseph Reners had already set sail to Charles Town.

Standing pensively on the quarterdeck that night, he lowered the flame of his deck lantern so his eyes could become accustomed to the starlight. Whatever anyone might say, he thought to himself, oblivious to the world over the horizon, turning forty was a landmark in a man's life that should not be contemplated alone, so he gazed up at the stars. Both his father and grandfather had drawn their last breath at sixty, which to Joseph meant that he might well be two-thirds through his own life already.

Perhaps it was time to change course, he thought, picking out his old companion, the North Star, as a warm Caribbean wind whistled through the creaking rigging. Anyway, he had quite had his fill of roving from port to port. It was not so much the ports he was jaded by, more the bits in-between, the seafaring bits which were either extremely dangerous or downright tedious. But on this voyage, he had a very important passenger, and he squeezed his hands silently together in anticipation of a coquetry, or even a pursuit of true love, if that was still possible at his time of life.

A strong leader and proud of his person, he had nonetheless made a success of his twenty years of roaming. He had recently purchased a larger vessel to ferry goods and chattel, and he had amassed a fair fortune. His line of business was not likely to flounder either. In fact, he had a notion that it was just the beginning.

But Captain Reners, during those bits between ports, more and more often got to thinking he had no family, no wife, no children. Perhaps it was time to settle down, make a home some place. He could hire a good captain to do the navigating, and besides, what with the hostilities in Europe, he sensed things were about to turn even choppier at sea.

It was two hours after sundown, and a near full moon now shimmered over a slight sea.

Then he heard it.

The creak of a cabin window.

He stealthily stepped to the starboard bulwark of his new merchant ship and leaned over. 'Good Lord,' he murmured, 'she's doing it again!'

He was not referring to his seventy-ton vessel that coasted at an even keel through the Windward Passage into the waters of the Bahamas. She was quite perfect and a beauty to behold—a far cry from his old pink—more navigable on long voyages, and she coursed through the wavelets like a bolt. No, he was referring to Madame Stuart, his very important passenger whose presence kept him well-groomed and smelling of lavender water.

Admittedly, he had been looking forward to his usual stopover at Nassau, until the governor of Saint-Domingue asked him to take aboard his widowed niece. It would be untoward to carry a lady of quality to such a riotous place.

He would have to put in elsewhere to water, which was a pity, because of all the lovely ladies he admired in all his ports of call, Betty was the loveliest of them all, and Betty was in Nassau. Soft and reassuring was Betty, motherly almost, and she had the softest bosom a weary gentleman traveller could lay his head upon. The perfect companion to help round the cape of your fortieth birthday.

But this youngish widow would do fine, he thought to himself rascally. He had already noted the worldliness of her glance, and he liked strong-willed women, ones capable of handling themselves.

He looked down the side of the hull again as *La Bella Fortuna* cut through the water. 'How strange,' he said to himself, as below him another dress was thrown out of the cabin window.

He had been considering how it would improve his status in higher circles to marry a governor's widowed niece . . . But was she, though? Was she really who she said she was? He was beginning to wonder . . .

'Cap'n, Sir,' said Mattis, a stocky matelot with a large, bullish head, standing at the foot of the poop-deck steps, 'I managed to pike this . . .' Reners twisted his torso to see the sailor holding up a beautiful crimson silk dress that gleamed in the night, the kind of dress Joseph had seen ladies wear in certain haunts of pleasure. He could barely hide his surprise. Who was Madame Stuart?

*

May Stuart had come a long way since leaving London all those years ago.

Sitting in the relatively comfortable cabin reserved for very important persons, she pulled out another wildly

3

expensive robe from the trunk she had placed beneath the glazed window. She held up the crimson garment of fine silk by the shoulders. 'Pity,' she said to herself, 'shan't be needing you anymore!' Then she pushed open the window and promptly bundled the robe through the dark hole into the star-speckled night.

Pulling out another alluring dress, she inwardly smiled at how easily she had the captain already eating out of the palm of her hand. She well knew the bovine-eyed look of a besotted middle-aged man. Yet, compared to the robe she was now holding up, she was very conservatively clad in a puritan black dress buttoned to the neck, with subtle white frills at the collar and sleeves. It contrasted forbiddingly with her copper blond hair and smooth, light skin. And her ruby-red lips stood out like an exquisite poppy in a field of barley. She did not need a dress to make her beautiful, she knew, but it was always reassuring when her beauty was confirmed. 'You can go too!' she said, and threw the robe she was holding out into the sparkling night.

She was relinquishing her costumes of seduction. And yet, as she swayed gently in time with the pitch of the ship, she had never felt more in command of her life.

The captain would be a fine catch for sure, she thought, if his ship was anything to go by. But May had already told herself she did not need a man to tell her what to do. She had had plenty of those already; none of them had been any good— except for her late husband, perhaps. But there again, she had been blinded by love, and thinking about it with hindsight, he had been no good either. He was the one who had lured her to the thrill of the voyage and the prospect of fortune, only to leave her caught in a never-ending cycle to make ends meet. From the French port of Saint Pierre to Spanish Havana, she had

4

exploited men's pillow talk and lifted their wallets, laced their drinks, and searched their pockets.

She pulled out another low-cut dress and threw it out. She had never intended to be a sinner, though. At least, not until she realised she was in possession of a formidable weapon. Some women were blessed with fabulous wealth from birth, others with a strong sense of motherhood; others still received the gift of caring, and some got nothing but ailments. As for May, the good Lord had provided her with beguiling beauty and irresistible sex appeal. Was it not her God-given right to exploit it for the sake of self-preservation? At least, it was the only way she had been able to navigate these shark-infested waters of man's new world.

'A new life. A new me,' she said to the glorious green dress she was holding up. Then she threw it out through the window.

At thirty-two, May felt like she had lived more lives than a bodega cat. But she had left Havana for good this time, and now she intended to be her true self. She had her little treasure and planned to invest in some land.

Sitting back in her chair, May imagined her new home, and what it would be like to live in four seasons again in the north. She pictured a pretty stone house with a roaring chimney in winter, a flowered garden, outhouses for storage of whatever she decided to invest in, a stable for a wagon and strong workhorses, a fine mare, and an upholstered French carriage with glass windows. But she could not yet picture a man. She would need one, of course, but what he would look like, she knew not. She only knew he would have to be dependable, as clever with his head as with his hands, and not lack etiquette. She would not fall for a fat-fingered merchant or a grubby-nailed tradesman, oh no: she wanted nothing less than a fine gentleman to be her partner through life. And she would spend the rest of it trying to be righteous and mending her soul; that is what she planned to do.

She would start by removing anything that reminded her of her past lives. But throwing away beautiful dresses was not as easy as she thought, and she had been obliged to stop the previous night. She could have sold them, or even given them away, but that would have been betraying her true self, not to mention the dresses. They had been like a second skin to her and had served her well. They had raised her profile and given her a certain standing. But if she was to seek redemption, she would have to part with them, to relegate them to the vault of her memory like past lovers.

She took another sip of rum, braced herself, and then threw out the offending dress.

After leaving Havana in her usual, more . . . uplifting attire, she had changed into something more appropriate once in Port-de-Paix. Here, the governor, in exchange for her intelligence services, had assured her of a passage aboard the merchantman headed north to Charles Town, Carolina, the new port town where she returned twice yearly.

She picked up the last robe but one left in the trunk, her second favourite. This time, after flinging it out, she poked her head through the window and watched the shimmering saffron dress sail away into the night like a phantom of her past. It suddenly occurred to her that someone could have spotted it as it momentarily floated up with the wind in the direction of the ship. But then it did a pirouette and tumbled blindly into the dark sea. Besides, who would be looking out into the night at this late hour? 'There,' she said, sitting back down in the armchair before her trunk, 'all gone, all but one, just in case . . .' and she gave a deep sigh.

TWO

IN ANOTHER SHIP faraway, Didier Ducamp was on morning watch.

He was swaying in his hammock and enjoying the solace of the soft breeze on the quarterdeck. This was the watch he liked best because he could snatch some private time under lamplight, and dip into that book he never thought he would ever hold again let alone read.

He had served as a dragoon lieutenant in the French army, but had become sick of being the cutting edge held to the throats of soft-bellied Protestants, known in France as Huguenots, to purge the nation of heretics. Heretics, that is, according to the king and clergy. Not that he was the religious type himself; his experience had long since shown him that all men bled the same when sliced, and one man's innards resembled another's, whether you rode with Jesus, Ol' Nick, or Neptune.

It was a Huguenot, a good man who had served on this ship as an indentured barber-surgeon, who had given him this Protestant Bible. It meant Ducamp could read the word of God in his own language as opposed to the obscure lingo of the clergy. And it was surprisingly simple, which only sharpened his scorn for those who enshrouded themselves in floating robes and mystic reverence because they could speak in Latin.

But as far as Didier was concerned, God was quite possibly the greatest impostor of them all. Didn't his sweet, God-fearing wife and child die of some God-given disease? And this, while he was busy "converting" more Huguenots to the "true" faith than the archbishop of Paris.

Besides, there was no point groping for Jesus on this godforsaken ship. Sailing under Captain Brook took care of that. More sinful a man there never was, and if Ducamp had known at the outset what he was signing into, maybe he would never have signed up. There again, maybe he would have. Either way, he would have been signing away his soul.

So instead of praying to Jesus, he, like most of the ragged crew, had been hoping for Lady Luck to change the course of their fortunes, for they had not encountered another ship in weeks. They had sailed north toward Charles Town but then, halfway up they had decided to swing the sloop around and enter the Windward Passage from the north. But they had come upon some rough westerly winds that had blown them further out to sea, which was nonetheless better than being pushed onto the coast of Florida, littered as it was with shifting sandbars. Ducamp was no navigator, but according to Johnny Reed at the helm, they should be approaching the Bahama Islands and heading for the Windward Passage.

But tacking southward in a westerly wind was slow. Provisions were running low. The hens no longer laid their cackle fruit, and what was left of the barrel of apples was turning to mush. The fat cow had already been slaughtered, and Hammond the cook had been caught doing abominable things to the chickens again before wringing their necks. The long and the short of it was that they desperately needed a sea encounter to replenish the hold.

Amazing, thought Ducamp to himself as he peeled his eyes from the prose on the page and laid down the book of God on his bare chest. He gazed into the stars. 'Is that what all the fuss is about? Thank the heavens for bloody baccy and rum!' he growled to himself and swiped a dram of kill-devil across his lips.

The promise of Christ did give him a moment of comfort, though, to imagine his dead wife and child in heaven, and not just dead and rotting in the mass grave outside the village he once called home. The book offered another dimension to life on earth, something to hope for in spite of dire misfortune. But it did not alter the fact that he was a sinner, a soldier, and now a privateer bosun, skilled in the art of killing, and now doing it for what he and every man on this ship worshipped more than anything: coin. He was condemned.

A breeze kissed his salty cheek and stirred the strands of hair that had escaped from his pigtail dowsed in pitch. Pitch kept his dark mop in one clump and out of his face in times of toil and war. He had become as inured to its sweet odour as he had to the foul-smelling bilge water down below deck.

Didier closed his book of God and carefully wrapped it in a sailcloth sack. He had gotten his fill of fabled gospels for one watch; now he had to keep focussed. This Windward Passage they were supposed to be entering was rife with game, which was why they would not be ploughing the sea any faster than a couple of knots, even if the wind changed direction. There was no point running in and straight out of these prime hunting waters, especially since the declaration of war between England and France. No, the problem was not contrary winds—it was lack of fair and legitimate game.

Captain Brook had acquired a letter of marque in Port Royal that gave them every right to take whatever French vessel they found. But it came with a caveat; it meant they were forbidden to take a Spanish ship should they encounter one, given that the Spanish were in league with the English in Europe against the French king. This world was decidedly mad, thought Didier.

Ducamp had long since lost all notion of patriotism. He had fought in King Louis's wars to bring back a livelihood for his wife. She had made an oasis of happiness amid his life of battlefields and desolation: a house, a babe, good food on the table, and a soft touch to his battle scars at night. But she was gone, the oasis was no more, and he felt neither attachment to king or country. He was a man with no home, an errant soul lost at sea. If he died now, no one would miss him.

Didier went about pacing up and down the main deck, making sure the lads of the morning watch still had their weather-eye peeled. There was a good hour yet before the sky would start to pale, the last chance to get a good view of the lights of any distant ship.

He paused at the port rail and defiantly cast his gaze into the night that supposedly enshrouded all the devil-made monsters of the deep blue sea. But Didier Ducamp did not believe in giant squids and mermaids, any more than he believed in trumpeting angels. Again he blinked and squinted into the darkness. And there it was again, a distant light twinkling like a star on the paling horizon. Then there came a loud, booming roar that broke the snoring cycles of men snatching a watch-worth of slumber—men curled up in alcoves or slung in hammocks from stern to bow.

'Ship ahoy! Ship ahoy!' belched Billy Hawke, perched up

in the high sails. 'South by southeast!' His powerful howl was enough to rouse the devil, and Ducamp could already hear Captain Brook snorting in his cabin nearby.

Better not be Spanish, thought Ducamp. He was not keen on getting hanged for piracy.

*

Captain Brook had a short fuse and a crowded mind. He had been unable to sleep, what with his ailment and Mulatto Joe being too ill to apply the treatment. So he had been obliged to apply his mercury unction to his facial and genital sores himself.

'Bugger off, I'm busy!' he snapped in reply to a knock at his door, and continued rinsing a cloth in a leather pail of water.

The knocker was not intimidated by the gruff response. Didier knew that withholding information from his captain would bring far greater wrath than rousing him at five in the morning.

'Ducamp, Cap'n. We got a ship in view.'

'Bloody well come in then, man,' replied Brook in a gravelly but lighter tone. A ship in view could mean a doctor aboard, or at least a medical chest. He was not the only man on the *Joseph* to think simultaneously of food, treasure, and medicine.

Ducamp yanked open the sticking door, his body filling the frame. He stepped into the eclectic and garishly furnished cabin that glowed with the light of beeswax candles in a leather lantern. It was hung over an acajou writing desk. To his right, the bosun was momentarily surprised to see the little mulatto lying in the captain's alcove bunk. Brook had pulled back the damask curtain and was placing a damp cloth on Joe's forehead.

'How is he?' said Ducamp without emotion.

'Needs a bloody doctor. We should never have let Delpech go,' replied Brook with a snarl.

Jacob Delpech was the barber-surgeon who had been released from his indenture for a price and the gift of the mulatto.

'Joe wouldn't be here if you hadn't,' said the bosun forthrightly. It was a privateer, a certain Captain Dugraaf, who had bought the indenture and had thrown in the mixed-race lad of nineteen to secure the deal, seeing that Brook had taken a shine.

'Aye, and I wouldn't be losing him now, would I!' returned the captain with a bitter smile which to Ducamp was no more readable than the man's permanent snarl. Yet, for a fleeting instant, the thought entered Ducamp's mind that Brook was concealing tenderness. But the bosun did not care enough to pursue it. Once he had obtained what he had joined the crew for, he would be off, off to start a new life, get himself some land in the south. He turned his gaze from Brook's deep-set eyes and hideously pockmarked face to the cabin port window.

'We've spotted a stern light south by southwest.'

'Aye, that's good . . .'

'Permission to snub out the lights, Cap'n.'

Ducamp turned back to face Brook, who shot a sharp look at the bosun and said: 'No, man, and I'll tell ya why. Chances are they've already spied us. Snuff out our lights now, and we become suspect, and we're too close to daylight to mount a night attack. Get me drift?' Ducamp gave a half nod. Brook continued. 'We got 'em on their starboard. The sun'll be behind us come daybreak. We'll see their colours before they see ours, savvy?'

Brook's quick assessment and his seafaring insight reminded Ducamp why he still had the command of this ship. That and his bloody ruthlessness which many a man would take for shear barbarity. No, a gentleman privateer Ned Brook was not, but a seaman and a hardnosed strategist he certainly was.

The captain continued: 'Then we hoist whatever be friendly to them,' he said, glaring into Ducamp's eyes, then adding as an afterthought: 'And pray to the devil it's bloody French, eh, bosun?' said the captain, and then he went back to dabbing Joe's forehead.

Ducamp knew how much Brook enjoyed the company of the mulatto, but seeing him like this was almost endearing, like watching a child stroke a cherished puppy. Did it suggest there was an ounce of humanity in the man yet? wondered Ducamp, backing out of the cabin, but he doubted it; then the thought was gone.

*

Two hours later, the Caribbean sun blazed down on the clear blue waters where the *Joseph* was coursing all sails set and flying a white French ensign.

The forty-two vigorous and desperate shipmates, having scoffed down their meagre ration of gruel washed down with a throatful of rumbullion, were crowded in front of the quarterdeck.

As per the ship's custom for major decisions, Captain Brook was addressing the men before putting his proposed course of action to the vote. Didier, standing beside him to his left, knew it was more a rabble-rousing formality than anything else but one which, according to the articles every man had signed, enabled the captain to take full and unconditional command of the imminent attack.

Brook had donned a French gold-braided frock coat with brass buttons. Quartermaster Blunt was impeccably dressed likewise and had covered his bald pate with a musketeer's tricorn hat for the hell of it, all to keep up false appearances should they be viewed from the long end of a spyglass. Ducamp did not need to pretend, clad as he was in his tattered French lieutenant's outfit. He had long since ceased to derive any pride from it, though. For this was a ship of men of all nations, men having stepped out from beneath the yoke of class and race to embrace the free-spirited life of a privateer. Although there had been times when some would have called them pirates. However, the news of war in Europe had thankfully brought them back into the realm of legality.

Brook could now brandish with triumph his letter of marque obtained in Port Royal, Jamaica. It allowed them to intercept and plunder French vessels without the risk of being hanged for piracy if caught. Yet, the governor had suggested he scour for French vessels in the Lesser Antilles, where French and English navies would be occupied defending dominions to protect their lucrative sugar plantations. But Brook had had a better idea than roving near the French navy fleet. He had deduced that French merchant plunder would be more easily had on the trade route from Port-de-Paix along the east coast of Florida and up to French Acadia in the north.

'She be a merchantman,' boomed Brook over the balustrade, 'flying merchant colours!' Then, pausing for effect while brandishing his letter of marque, he bayed: 'And she be French, me mates!'

There arose a cohesive roar of assent from the men standing before him, clambered high on rigging, or perched on the yardarms as sure as sprogs on a tree, despite the increasing swell.

Brook continued. 'And 'e who says merchantman says easy pickings, by thunder. Am I right, lads?'

Ducamp, like most of the men, could but agree to the assumption, for why else would she be headed northward if it were not for trade? But most of all, she flew the blue-and-white merchant ensign of New France.

Ducamp looked down on the deck, where one man with a barrel of a chest raised a thick, brawny arm. It was Jack Cooper, the master carpenter. Before the roars had died down, he bawled out: 'Aye, but I say she looks mightily armed for a merchantman, Cap'n, like she could put up a fair fight!'

'She might be armed, and even if she is, man, I ask youse, mates, have you ever seen in your all miserable lives a bunch of merchant sailors risk their necks for a sailor's wage?' said Brook, leaning over the rail. 'Come what may, she'll surrender as soon as we hoist our colours, I say. What say you, lads? Are youse with your ol' Cap'n Brook?' The ensuing uproar of confidence wiped away any lingering doubt. 'Besides, where else we gonna find fresh meat, medicine, and water in this sea-salty world, eh?' said Brook who knew he had hit a soft spot on implicitly referring to everyman's ailment. For even if the brigantine doctor refused to step forward, at least they would probably be able to get their hands on medical supplies.

Blunt, the quartermaster, put the imminent attack to the vote, which to no one's surprise came back with a unanimous raising of hands in favour of the chase. It may have been a formality, but Ducamp knew as well as Captain Brook that the articles had to be respected to keep up the appearance of democracy aboard, or else they ran the risk of being deposed.

'And remember, lads,' called out the deep-chested voice of the quartermaster, 'we wants her crew alive so we can weed out the doctor!'

'And I want me a new ship,' blustered the captain, 'so let's keep destruction to a minimum, and we'll soon be sailing the high seas in style. Wouldn't that be nice, me wily wolves!' concluded the captain, which met with another collective roar interspersed with wild hoots and howls.

*

At the same moment, on the ten-gun brigantine, the *Beaufort,* Captain Chancre was conferring with his officers.

He had been secretly missioned by the governor of Saint-Domingue to investigate the veracity of a shipwreck, supposedly a Spanish payroll ship, off the east coast of Florida. That explained why he had set sail under a merchant standard of blue and white. Reinforcements were to follow should Governor de Cussy receive further intelligence from another source. It was not unheard of for the Spanish to plant false information to lure their enemy away from sensitive points, such as the Lesser Antilles, a known target for conquest.

'She shows French navy colours, Sir,' said the first officer to the captain.

'A king's ship she certainly is not, though,' returned Captain Chancre. Having removed his spyglass from his left eye, he snapped it shut. 'A privateer at best, by the looks of the rabble on the quarterdeck. They are, however, in French uniform.'

'It might be a ploy, Sir,' said a young second officer.

'I doubt that, Monsieur de Blanc. They have been keeping up the rear since the early hours. She is a sloop, a good three knots faster than this brigantine. Why would they reveal themselves when they might well have crept up under cover of the night?'

'To verify our colours, Sir?'

'Should that be the case, then we shall reserve her a rip-roaring surprise. But no, I suspect she is an envoy from the governor.' Indeed, if de Cussy had received extra intelligence, he would certainly have sent a fast runner to confirm the whereabouts of the precious wreckage before the Spanish raised a salvage force in Havana.

Captain Chancre dismissed First Mate de Blanc and gave the command to keep the ship's course.

THREE

DIDIER DUCAMP PASSED his eyes over a handful of fellow shipmen going about their mariners' duties with diligence, in the sails and on deck.

The rest of the rabble, having prepped their arms and smudged their faces with blackening from burnt wood, were lying lined up like mackerel below the raised bulwark, out of sight of the prying spyglass. Five swivel guns mounted on the gunwale were primed in case of resistance, and a warning shot packed into an eight pounder was loaded in wait port side on the prow deck.

However, nine times out of ten, Didier knew that their blood-curdling roars and dreadful appearance would be enough to put the fear of the devil into any good man who sailed under the thumb of a merchant captain. Most of them would surrender and some even take the raid as an opportunity to jump ship, fed up as they usually were with a captain's harsh treatment and a miserable life on low pay.

It was nonetheless a deadly game of cat and mouse that could cost lives. If resistance there be, Ducamp had, however, managed to persuade Brook to make a point of letting a man live to tell the story if he surrendered. And nine times out of ten, that was what they did. It was good for the crew's reputation and let future prey know their lives would be spared if they gave up the fight.

The mid-afternoon had turned gusty, and clouds were bubbling in the purpling sky as the *Joseph* closed behind the brigantine, now no further than a cable length ahead. The sea had grown and, given the present squall, the brigantine had reefed her sails, considerably reducing her speed. It came as no surprise to Ducamp when Brook, on the other hand, gave the command to show more canvas. It was a clever manoeuvre, one that would reduce the advantage of the brigantine's firepower. For it allowed the nimble sloop to swiftly billow up close to the prey so that, if the larger ship fired, her cannon would be too high to aim into the sloop's belly.

As another rise of the swell brought the *Joseph* level with the brigantine's rear deck, Brook blurted out: 'Piss pot! Hell's bloody bells!'

In the same instant, Ducamp saw a flurry of bonneted men file from the brigantine's hatchways as their captain advanced proudly to the quarterdeck starboard bulwark. He then stood with his back arched while the white flag was hoisted at the stern before him.

'Shiver me liver, these ain't no merchants!' growled Brook.

'No, it's the bloody French navy, Cap'n!' returned the quartermaster as the white navy standard now unfurled on the stern pole of the brigantine.

It occurred to Didier that the only rational course of action would be to let the wind out of the sails, drop back, and scoot away in the opposite direction. But Brook was already fired up. He had that glazed-over feral look in his eye, and now his nostrils widened as he fleetingly assessed the navy men. Ducamp sensed their inexperience, too, as

19

they positioned themselves in an orderly fashion behind the French ship's bulwark.

Meanwhile, Captain Chancre composedly brought a megaphone to his mouth to request the latest intelligence from Port-de-Paix. But before he could open it, the supposed emissary grinned maliciously and hurled out in English: 'Hoist our colours, lads!' Chancre watched in horror as the English ensign was being raised, and along the bulwark, a rabble of cutthroats reared their blackened faces while brandishing muskets, pikes, pistols, and cutlasses and hurling a thousand threats of anatomic destruction. Some rattled their sabres, their eyes huge; others stared steadfast, their tongues playing on their blades, their features projecting an intent to do evil.

The *Joseph* was now level with the brigantine's quarterdeck broadside. Leaning over the balustrade, Captain Brook boomed out to the French commander. 'Surrender, Cap'n. You are outnumbered! We only want your medicines and victuals,' he hollered, lying by omission. In fact, he had spent the entire afternoon ogling the brigantine's every curve through his spyglass, figuring how he could make her more powerful. He had even consulted the ship's carpenter on the feasibility of his plans. He would unclutter the decks, make space for ten more guns on each side, and raise the gunwale for protection. He had measured how gracefully she furrowed the sea, how high and mightily she cut through the swelling waves, and he was intent on getting his heart's desire. It was indeed time to scale up, he thought. The men, too, were keen on riding the waves in more space and style.

'Never!' returned an infuriated Captain Chancre in French. 'I will blow you scoundrels to kingdom come!'

Ducamp acted as interpreter. 'He don't seem to like the idea,' he said.

'Then tell 'im we'll send a more persuasive message,' said Brook and made a sign to Quartermaster Blunt, standing on the main deck with a gun team. No sooner had Ducamp finished his translation than a terrifying blast rent the air and an eight-pound cannonball went hurtling over the brigantine's deck, causing many a French navy sailor to dive for cover. It was increasingly clear to Ducamp that some of these men had never seen action.

'Warning shot!' boomed Brook from the sloop. 'Now, last chance, Cap'n!'

Captain Chancre was momentarily taken aback by the sheer audacity of the villains. But he quickly composed himself, assured in the knowledge that his vessel was twice the size of the sloop, and had three times the firepower.

But the sloop was twice as populated with desperados used to killing, and who knew full well that this might be their last chance to take on fresh supplies. Brook knew the sloop was also more nimble, and what steeled the privateer's most was her keel being lower than the row of cannons that now pointed their muzzles out of the brigantine's gun deck. The bigger vessel might blow away the sloop's mast, but the buccaneers would take the brigantine for sure if they could sling their grappling hooks. If they got close enough to board, the ship was theirs.

All too aware of this, Captain Chancre gave the order to veer to larboard in an attempt to peel away from the dogged sloop and realign from a distance. It was the only way he could blow these pesky raiders out of the water.

However, Brook and his crew had played through these motions before, though never with a navy ship, and yet, it was all too predictable. 'Keep her close, lads, and she be ours!' thundered the captain while the sloop raced along the rear starboard flank, stealing the wind from the lower sails of the taller ship. 'Are we not sea dogs, me hearties!' he roared at the bow as they raced like a lynx after the larger prey. 'Fire at will, lads,' he called up to the men in the sails. 'Keep the lubbers off the deck!' Then, turning to the bosun and the hoard of hell's hounds that lined the main deck below, he bellowed: 'Fire at high water!'

Ducamp, with a finger on his musket trigger in anticipation of the rise of the sea, led the fire, which was instantly followed by a volley of accompanying shots. He was thankful to see his target grasp his arm, not his heart, as the sloop dipped again with the roll of the sea below the rail of the brigantine. Lucky it did, too, thought Ducamp, now crouching below the gunwale with the men for cover. The brigantine had followed up with a thunderous salvo of cannon fire that went hurtling clean over the bow spit, punching holes in the sails. A rigger was hit, fell, and dropped to the deck like a dead turkey, but the mast remained standing.

The sloop edged further up the starboard aft of the larger ship, while the buccaneers on deck kept up successive volleys of musket fire, pinning down the outnumbered French sailors.

'Grapples away!' thundered Brook, now seeing the window of opportunity as the two ships came hull to hull. 'Cast the grapples before she gives more sail!'

Another dexterous swing of the rope, and the predator had its claws firmly clutching its prey. Ducamp, amid the melee of roaring men, sensed the end was nigh. He hoped it would turn out like it did nine times out of ten, that this time, there would be no need to put any lambs to the slaughter to win the submission of the flock. Nine times out of ten, if it were not for Brook's innate thirst for blood, he knew it would. However, the captain appeared to be in a more calculating frame of mind this afternoon because this ship he wanted for his own.

'Keep 'em off the deck, lads, till we've boarded!' cried out Blunt next to Ducamp, while Captain Brook positioned himself behind the swivel gun mounted at the sloop's bow. He did not want any clumsy lubber pummelling his new ship.

'I got the lascars!' he roared, seeing a famed victory over the French in his sights, while motioning to the men to begin the ascent on the trailing ropes. 'First man aboard gets an extra share!' he bayed as Harry, the lithe rigger, deft with a blade, led the surge. Jack Cooper, the burly carpenter, was close on the rigger's heels. No doubt they, too, had sensed the reticence and inexperience of these fresh sailors unused to killing.

But if this battle were to go down in history, it would be for a reason which would make Brook regret firing the swivel gun as the ship pitched and rose again.

The captain took aim at the navy sharpshooters positioned behind the brigantine's bulwark, desperately priming their pistols for another volley into the melee of clambering men. On the rise of the swell, he blasted a bore-load of grapeshot to scatter the bastards. It would do only superficial damage to the ship, but would scatter the enemy and clear the way for his men to climb over the gunwale and board.

Brook was already warming to the idea of taking possession of his new ship when another musket shot whizzed past his right ear and sunk into the mast behind him with a dull thud. By thunder, he really did have the luck of the devil; aye, he was invincible, he thought, now pulling out his cutlass

23

to join the melee and perform delicious wickedness in all legality before the surrender was pronounced.

But as he did so and the sloop dipped beneath the brigantine's rail, there came a bright flash from above. It was immediately followed by an appalling, air-splitting blast that rumbled through every fibre of timber of the sloop, hull to hull as it was with the brigantine. Brook dived for cover beneath the gunwale as great splinters of wood showered over the deck like shards of glass. Another flash, and an even more horrific explosion followed, a gut-churning blast of damnation if ever there was.

Most of the privateers were still climbing onto the trailing ropes along the hull as the blast went off, luckily clean over their heads. They sprang back like a horde of spiders suddenly fleeing their prey as the sloop lowered into the trough of a wave. Only Harry the rigger and Jack Cooper the carpenter had made it to the brigantine's bulwark. Quartermaster Blunt looked up to take stock of the loss of lads. He was not usually so caring, but he was sworn into matelotage with one of the climbers, which meant, should the matelot get himself killed, the quartermaster would inherit his stash. But as he scoured the faces of the men scrambling down, a fine shaft of timber came bolting out of the murky blue and sank neatly between his eyes. He staggered around the deck with the stumped look of a drunken sailor until at last, being a shipshape and neat-minded man, he stumbled toward the starboard and toppled clean over the bulwark into the frothing sea.

Captain Brook turned to Ducamp, who had scrambled back into the sloop on the second detonation. 'Bloody ship's magazine!' he hollered above the din of falling debris and the cries of men. The brigantine's timbers cracked loudly. Brook and Ducamp quickly got to their feet as an arm landed next to them. Shielding his head with his forearms, the bosun instinctively looked up, and, in the blink of an eye, he recognised Harry's pitched and plaited head hurtling toward them. It would have killed them as good as a cannonball had he not had the reflex to step back and push Brook aside in time to let the head bound off the decking.

'Man overboard!' someone shouted further along in reference to another mate having fallen. The timing made Ducamp snort with fleeting amusement as Harry's head ended its course in the sea. Then, recovering from the moment, he turned to the frantic escape of those who had gotten higher up the trailing ropes. Grabbing men by the scruffs of their necks, he helped haul them back over the sloop's gunwale. 'Fire in the sails!' someone else shouted as the enemy ship let out another sickening crack. She was breaking up, and Ducamp saw the immediate danger. He rushed along the line of recovering men, shouting out: 'Leave the fire. Cut away the grapples! Man the oars!'

He tried not to think about the appalling cries of men burning alive on the brigantine. Then, the whole massive ship gave a loud lurching sound as the incessant stress of the pummelling sea was splitting her hull asunder.

By now, the sloop crew were pulling hard on the oars. The battle was over, and it left Ducamp with a sickly feeling, a soul-scathing sentiment which he desperately wanted to reverse. He stood paralysed a moment as the Frenchmen on the brigantine, his countrymen, were crying out to God and their mothers for help.

In his turmoil, he grabbed Mali the Mint to help him set free the sloop's gig. This way, at least those who could be saved could find a refuge.

'What you doin', man?' growled a voice behind his ear amid the terrible din. Ducamp turned and saw Brook.

'We can't just leave them, man. They'll drown!'

'We can and we will. They're already dead, man, and you'll be joining them if you try to help them now. When she goes down, there'll be one hell of a wave that'll pound down upon us like Neptune's arse . . . We gotta get away, man . . . Fast . . . so take up an oar!'

They were pulling hard and barely thirty yards from the brigantine when Ducamp saw her extremities bob up in the choppy waves as she split in the middle. And then she slipped down to the depths of the sea. Great mounds of air exploded to the surface, and quickly developed into a colossal wave. It welled up and rolled outward from its epicentre, and began bowling toward the sloop.

'Christ! Shut the ports! Batten the hatches!' boomed Ducamp.

Too late. Seconds later, seawater went gushing into the lower decks, filling the hold, pushing the cannons to starboard, and causing the ship to list. Five degrees more and she would have followed the French brigantine to the seabed.

It was an odd time to choose, but Ducamp knew then he did not want to die this way—a sinner, a killer of men— with a scathed soul.

The great wave swept over the deck, its glutinous fingers reaching as high as the top yards, and washed most of the fires out.

*

By late afternoon, the storm had blown away, and the sky had grown clear again. Ducamp sat with a handful of mates, exhausted, starving, and battered, on the quarterdeck still strewn with splinters and body parts from the explosion. They had spent hours manning the pumps and changing the canvas that had been devoured by flames.

Brook stepped out of his cabin; it had relieved him to find Joe unchanged despite all the commotion. Turning to Ducamp, the captain said: 'Pity, a real booty, weren't she!'

Ducamp's eyes flitted at the neighbouring mates. Then he looked at the captain with a jerk of incredulity. The man really was insane. 'We've just destroyed a shipload of men,' he said.

'Aye, and we'll be needing another carpenter!' returned Brook, who picked up a burly arm and lobbed it into the sea.

While Brook had retired to tend to his mulatto, some of the men had been grousing about the lack of prey, no pay and no food. 'Is the explosion a sign from God?' one of them had asked. 'Are we all now paying for Brook's past barbarities?' another had wondered. But then a cry from the sails changed their tune.

'Ship ahoy!' cried out a rigger in the crow's nest.

You lucky bastard! thought Ducamp to himself as he turned to Captain Brook. Then he said to him: 'You really do have the luck of the devil, Cap'n!'

FOUR

CAPTAIN RENERS STEPPED below deck as the night navigator called out a reminder to the helmsman: 'Steady as she goes!'

In the dark stern passageway, the merchant captain's eyes fell upon the sliver of light below Madame Stuart's cabin door.

May lingered an instant in the armchair by the window, examining her options now that she had at last secured the means required to enable her to break away from her sinful past. She was so much looking forward to reuniting with her young daughter, Lili-Anne, who she had placed with Mrs Moore. A childless widow, Helen Moore ran a boarding home for children of settlers who were obliged to travel for reasons of work. May hoped and prayed that nothing untoward had come to the child since she had seen her last, which was before the hurricane season. But what if she had fallen ill, had been a victim of an accident? May turned away from the window, daring not to enter that dark tunnel of thought. 'Of course my lil' Lily-Anne is well,' she told herself, blotting out any nasty deliberations that served no other purpose than to make her worry. For there was nothing she could do except make sure the child was well provided for, that she would be as precious to her wet nurse as to her mother.

The nightwatchman called out his usual plaintive lament, like a sigh in the night: 'Steady as she goes!' Then a sharp knock at the door snapped May from her introspections.

Standing on the other side of the cabin door, Captain Reners squashed his nose into the intoxicating silk fabric of the beautiful perfumed dress. It was the perfume of both a romantic ideal and of love lost before it had been allowed to blossom. Yet, how absurd, he thought to himself, that at his time of life, one could still feel cheated in love. But cheated he did feel, cheated of the redemption of a misspent life, of the chance to at last found a family. He sometimes wondered where he would be now had he made space in his busy schedule, going back and forth across the ocean. However, at least there was the consolation of the fleeting pleasure of a physical encounter, wasn't there? He was about to find out.

May quickly laid down her favourite gown in her trunk, which she quietly closed.

'Madame Stuart?' said the captain in a low voice. 'It is Captain Reners. Are you all right?' Then he rolled up the dress sailor-fashion and wedged it inside his frock coat under his arm.

May got up from her chair and stepped across the narrow cabin. She prodded her fine auburn hair, straightened her puritan dress, and opened the door.

'Yes, Captain, quite all right,' she said, offering a genteel smile.

'Ah,' returned the captain, whose relief at her coming to the door was genuine. 'I noticed your light. All is well, I trust?'

'Thank you, Captain, as well as any sea voyage can be, I dare say. I . . . I was about to turn in, actually.'

'Good,' he said. May did not fail to notice a new glint in his eye. He continued: 'I would not like your uncle to hear of any . . . discomfort.'

'My uncle?' returned May, her mind still in the fogginess of her introspection. She had almost forgotten her cover, but in the next instant, she said: 'Oh, yes, my uncle. Why would he?'

Joseph gave a condescending smile. 'May I?' he said, delicately pushing the door in his stride, and walked into the candlelit, room made more agreeable thanks to an array of fabrics placed here and there over the chair and upon the luggage along the left-side wall going in. It was a far cry from the squalor and stench below deck, where men constantly groaned like beasts, thought the captain. In here, the colours and the mellow candlelight were positively inebriating.

'Are you planning on moving permanently to Charles Town, if you don't mind my asking?' said Joseph Reners, motioning to the luggage stacked along the partition wall of the cabin and encompassing the trunk below the window. She had preferred to keep her belongings with her rather than have them stored in the hold. He gazed back unflinchingly, taking in her exquisitely smooth forehead, the signs of age encroaching around her candid eyes that somehow enhanced her sensuality, and her dainty mouth.

Her large eyes smiled knowingly at his misplaced regard. Was the captain about to declare his flame? she wondered. If he did, she would have three long weeks to find out about his financial affairs. Could he be the husband she required? Nevertheless, she gave a straight-lipped smile and, hand on hip, she said affably: 'Captain, what is it that you want?'

He finished entering and softly closed the door after him. Then, turning to her, he said: 'I thought I would give you back something you have lost.' May tried to disguise her surprise with a cultured smile. But then her heart missed a beat when he pulled her crimson dress from inside his frock coat. 'Does this belong to you, by any chance?' he said with false candour as he unfurled the beautiful low-cut dress that shimmered in the candlelight.

'Oh,' said May, her eyes growing even wider. She could hardly deny it in the middle of the sea. She had been careless. She had to think quickly. 'Why, yes, or rather, no, it was given to me by an acquaintance before she died . . . I didn't think it appropriate to keep. But what of it?'

Reners moved with sudden speed to the trunk beneath the window before May could even think of preventing him. In the same movement, he slung the dress on the timber-framed rope bed that sagged in the middle and pulled open the heavy wooden trunk lid that May had not had time to lock. 'And this?' said Reners, clasping a fistful of May's favourite dress. Again, she had been careless, and she now found herself on the back foot.

'How dare you, Sir!' she said as her bright green eyes, flecked with gold hardened in annoyance. 'My uncle shall know about your intrus—'

'Your uncle?' interrupted Reners with an ironic chortle. 'Your uncle or your client?'

'What do you mean, Sir?'

'Your French is excellent; my compliments. Your cut-glass accent offers a perfect cloak for your, shall we say, coarser origins.'

'How dare you!'

'For you, Madame, are no more a fine lady than I am a

crown prince of England!' He spoke delicately and with amiability. He was in perfect control. 'You are a whore, my dear.'

Captain Reners was evidently an old hand. May would have to change tactics. She had nonetheless achieved her goal of securing a passage on the only French ship headed for Charles Town. What with the current hostilities in Europe, that was a feat in itself. Captain Reners must be carrying very important merchandise, she had deduced, only later to realise he was transporting slaves intended to be shipped on to Virginia. Now, to avoid any trouble with the authorities on arrival and to string the captain along, she would have to come clean. This way, she would be able to drop her fine-lady act and deploy her hard-earned virtues to win him over.

'All right, Captain Reners,' she said, arching her chest, 'the governor is not my uncle. And yes, he is a client of sorts, but not what you think. I pass intelligence to him from Havana . . . But I am not a whore,' she concluded with a self-assured smile in her voice.

'Then what is this for?' he said, holding out the pretty robe.

'That is a relic of a life when I entertained high-ranking gentlemen of influence, Captain.'

'I maintain you are a . . .'

'A retired courtesan, Sir, who moreover has feelings,' said May, with an indulgent pout and a frown that pleated her smooth forehead. She sensed the captain was about to become prey to desire. But as long as she kept him at arm's length, she would be able to string him along with the promise, albeit a false promise, of a more romantic bond.

'Once a courtesan, always a courtesan,' said Reners.

How pompous, thought May. Did he not know that

women forced themselves to do things for gain too? But she sensed he was about to become daring and perhaps lose his sense of propriety. If she did not fend him off now at the height of his flame, there was a high risk of rape, and once the realisation of his crime sank in, she knew full well the high likelihood of her becoming "lost" at sea so as to remove the victim and thus erase the crime.

He said: 'Not that I mind, though. In fact, I don't mind at all.' Reners, both thrilled and eroticised, seized her by the hand. His manhood manifested itself firmly in his loins, and he was proud to show her he still had it in him to take a pretty woman. 'What about some entertainment for the main man?' he purred in her ear.

'Captain, please,' protested May, trying to slip her hand out of his. 'Those days are behind me.'

But the lovely lady was warm and soft. Having stepped into that space allocated to intimacy, Joseph Reners now enlaced her with his lavender-scented embrace. Was there a better way to spend one's birthday?

She ducked and broke away. 'Please, Captain, do control yourself . . .' But there was, of course, no place to go. 'I might have once entertained in high society, but no gentleman has ever thrown himself upon me,' she lied. May knew she would have to choose between being a victim or taking the lead. She knew too well that men preyed on weakness and lack of confidence. 'Pray, Captain, I am fatigued tonight. Let us resume our discussion in the morning,' she said, taking his hand from her waist again and leading him to the door.

Joseph was not one to let go without a kiss, however. She let him find her cheeks with his lips. This was a mistake because then he placed them on her mouth, and pushed in his tongue until it found hers. Under different circumstances, she might have found it pleasing, but as he squeezed her plump breast and pressed himself against her thigh, she curled her fingers into rigid claws. Then she clasped her assailant by his swollen balls, her wrist sensing the stiff prick that preceded them.

Joseph let out a surprised yelp of pleasure and then one of pain as she dug in, and a sense of injustice invaded his being. First, he had been cheated out of his romantic love for a fine lady, and now, he was being deprived of his just consolation from a whore. He let fly a smart backhand which struck May's cheek, making her fall onto the bed.

Roused and frustrated, he was about to follow through to take what he was owed. But having slipped her hand through a hip-slit in her dress, May reached into her pocket and pulled out a sheathed dagger.

'Don't take offense, Captain,' she said, yanking the dagger from its sheath, 'but I think this will calm your ardour!'

'Hah, do you know how to use it, even?' he said in amused scorn.

'Come a step closer, and you shall find out!'

Reners searched her eyes to gauge the level of her determination. A whore would know how to take care of herself, and this one was no different. But it would not take much to overpower her. He could use the beautiful dress to protect his hand. But then, from the depths of the ship's hull, there came the haunting sound of a man wailing. Then someone knocked at the cabin door.

'Captain! We've another deaden.' Reners recognised the voice of Mattis, the sailor who had recovered the dress using his pike. He was a loyal, boot-licking member of the crew, an invaluable shipmate to have at sea and one who had followed Reners from the Bay of Toulon to the Gulf of St Lawrence. 'Bringing him up right now,' said Mattis through the door.

Reners stood to, lust turning to anger. 'Damn, that's the third in two days!' he let out, turning to the door. At this rate, he could well end up in Charles Town with nothing to sell but the barrels of cocoa, sugar, and spice. Then he gave a look to May, now on her feet with her hand on hip, having thrown down the sheath, and still holding her knife.

'If you will excuse me, Madame,' he said in a more composed manner. 'We shall have to take up our little conversation later, if you will.'

'Thank you for your visit, Captain,' said May, playing along. She had managed to hold out this time, but now, she would have to find some way of humouring this man, for she could hardly run away.

That woman is maddening, thought Reners as he strutted out of the cabin and followed Mattis to the lower deck, where a young black corpse was being taken away. Whores were supposed to read a man's intentions, know how to cater to a man's carnal appetites, weren't they? he said to himself. 'Throw him overboard, Pineau,' he said cantankerously to the master gaoler. 'And what's that bloody wailing?'

'His father, Sir, from what I gather.'

'Make him stop. Then I want the sick segregated. Remove the chickens, and put all the grey-looking Negroes at the bow. Tell the cook to prepare their gruel with the juice of half a lemon per head.' It was a remedy Reners had picked up during the course of his sea travels and which had saved more than a few lustreless slaves. He usually administered the remedy closer to port, to give the chattel back their sheen in time for market.

The dimly lit scene contrasted starkly with May Stuart's colourful, glowing cabin: the dank and the squalor, the reek of piss, the sound of chains and the groans of distress. It was not very pleasant, but to Captain Reners, it was the smell of money. He was transporting fifty-two blacks from Africa which he had purchased in Port-de-Paix. It was a big personal investment, for previously, he had only carried slaves for slaver merchants who took the lion's share. So tonight, he thought to himself, he would have to let his very important passenger settle. Moreover, being of a professional disposition, she was bound to come round to his way of thinking, and things would be that much more agreeable. So he was glad in one way he was able to turn away his anger before he did something he might regret, and it would allow her to sleep on it. And besides, she would be there tomorrow, and the next day; in fact, for the next three weeks, he would have her all to himself. They say that having a woman onboard a ship was a curse, thought Reners, but this voyage was looking to be one of the most pleasurable he had undertaken yet.

Right now, he set his mind to the difficult task of pointing out under lamplight which slaves were grey and which looked fit enough. Then a thought struck him, 'By the blood of Christ!' he said to himself, 'why, of course she refused. A courtesan has a price...' He could have kicked himself for being such an oaf; too much time being with lowly sailors, no doubt. He would rectify his error in the morning. Right now, however, he had to take care of his livelihood and remove the rotten apples so they would not infect the rest.

*

May awoke at first light, having slept fully clothed, with her dagger in hand and with a loaded muff pistol tucked under the straw-filled pillow.

She had spent much of the night wondering how she could hold the captain off. Surely, it would be impossible throughout the whole duration of the voyage. Or would it?

The first rays of the sun that dazzled off the waves found her sifting through her luggage pile. She then brought out a travelling medicine chest which she had purchased in Havana. With the key tucked into her corsage, she opened the little box that contained an assortment of medicinal vials. 'There,' she said to herself, if only she could induce him to sleep, or better still, remove his capacities for the remainder of the voyage. She sat on the stool before the small table, translating the labels from Spanish. At last, she found the one that contained belladonna. She took out the little glass vial from its compartment and clenched it in her hand with a certain glee. But then her brow crinkled under thought. 'Just one problem,' she said to herself. 'How will I pour it into his drink?'

However, five minutes later, as the warmth of the full sun began to make the timbers creak and smell of pitch, she heard a call that would carry with it a change of rules.

Again the sailor in the rigging called out: 'Ship ahoy!' And now, peering out across the great expanse of ocean, she could see the silhouette of a vessel heading toward them.

FIVE

DIDIER DUCAMP HAD been keeping watch on deck since daybreak.

He had sensed the crew were in sombre spirits from the death of three mates, and the loss of their plunder and food. Were it not for the back-to-back sighting of another French vessel southeast and heading north up the Florida coast, he sensed there might well have been mutiny in the air. But the sight of the merchantman the previous evening had trained the collective focus on imminent spoils, grub and grog. Aye, ole Brook had the luck of the devil, all right, thought Didier.

They had been trailing her stern light all night long, having left their own stern lamp extinguished. The weather had eased, although the westerly was still moderate, and the watchmen had resorted to using dark lanterns for manoeuvres, though most sailors knew the rigging blindfold. Repetition had made good seamen of them. But the westerly winds excluded the possibility of a night attack. Moreover, the sloop's timbers were sodden from the flooding after the incident of the sinking brigantine, and she had turned sluggish.

Brook had given the order to veer eastward with the wind

so the sloop could tack toward the merchant ship from the northeast. Standing with the sun on his back, Ducamp could now appreciate the advantage procured by the shrewd manoeuvre, for now it allowed the privateers to approach their prey from out of the dazzling morning sunshine.

Half an hour later, Ducamp was standing with the men facing the quarterdeck. Brook had tried the gentle approach; now he decided to do things the usual way. He said: 'No messing this time, lads. We bear down on her at full sail, lay ourselves alongside the lubbers. If she squirms, we hit her hard with cannon and swivels, round her aft, and board in the smoke! Are yer with me?' The mates let out a loud cheer.

*

Captain Reners of the *Bella Fortuna* had been alerted of the sloop during a restless sleep after the events of the night.

He never enjoyed committing a body to the watery depths, albeit that of a slave. It invariably gave him dark and clingy nightmares of his own demise. But he had long since learnt to deal with it, and now, standing on the quarterdeck in the bright morning light, he was quick to shake off the macabre feeling. After all, disposing of the cadavers before they began to fester was in the interest of all aboard. Keeping cadavers on board a ship would only risk the spread of disease, but it would also cause a wasting sickness of the slaves' minds and turn them black as molasses. Burial at sea might be hard on relations, but it was best practice.

Added to the morbid feeling was the appalling nervousness in the pit of his belly. If he should keep losing his investment at the present rate, then he would be severely out of pocket. He was beginning to regret being tempted to put down his own coin for this voyage. He began to suspect that these slaves had only recently arrived from Africa on a gruelling journey across the ocean. If they had not been given time to recover at Port-de-Paix, they would have been weak even before setting sail to Charles Town.

Reners usually transported Negroes for a client and then took a minimum price and a cut after the sale at the port of destination. But now that he had a sizeable ship, he had purchased fifty-two of the beggars in the belief that, according to Governor du Cussy, in case hostilities escalated into war in Europe, every enemy ship would be navigating the waters around the Caribbean sugar islands of St Kitts and Nevis. The coast north would be clear.

He was beginning to think he should have waited until he had replenished his capital after the recent purchase of his vessel. Both ship and chattel represented the greatest part of his hard-earned fortune. Losing an excessive number of slaves would set him back in his finances. Indeed, if the present death rate persisted, he might be obliged to sell the ship at a loss. How horrible that would be, he thought to himself, and at his age. So he had stayed up to see that the sickly slaves were segregated and their diet adjusted accordingly. It might seem a little premature to start worrying to the extreme, but he had a terrible gut feeling that this voyage could cost him dearly.

But for now, his mind was divided between the sloop closing in to pass them by, and the prospect of female company later on. All was not doom and gloom, he told himself, watching wary-eyed as the sloop approached at full sail, barely a cable-length away.

'She's a French sloop,' he said to Mattis.

'Aye, unless she's a trickster,' returned the latter, as light footsteps on the deck steps made both men wheel round to find themselves facing May Stuart.

'Ah, Madame Stuart,' said the captain, falsely affable, 'I trust you slept well.' Mattis, with a smug smile, gave the captain a nod and discreetly slipped away.

'Thank you, Captain Reners,' returned May with an equal degree of insincerity, 'I trust you had a pleasant night too?'

'I only regret my being called away,' he said, then lowered his voice. 'I was about to make you an offer, Madame—'

'Oh, well, before you go any further, Captain, I wish to rectify any misgivings you may have regarding my honour.'

'Your honour, Madame? Hah, and how might that fit in with the life of a courtesan? Don't they keep it in their . . . corsage?'

'Even if once I did, I would venture to say that it is worthier than keeping it in the hull of a slave ship, Captain. I heard the awful cries of chained men. Is that what you call honour?'

'Fear not, Madame, I never said I was big on honour. But I do have a large fortune . . .'

What a loathsome, arrogant braggart, thought May to herself. And to think she once wondered if he was of the marrying sort. He would no doubt have loved her and left her the moment he was done. May did not want to fall back into her life of old, the very one she was trying to escape. No, this was not what she wanted. She still had the upper hand, however, and she could string him along as long as she kept her virtue. Men with money thought themselves irresistible. Often, the trick was to bring them down a peg so they kept a foot in the real world, and henceforth adhereed to real-world etiquette. Many a time she had made a man check his step so he would consider her as a woman first instead of a mere object of desire. She knew that what she was about to ask would most likely not be met with approval, but at least she hoped her request would bring Reners back from the brink of disrespectfulness. If this did not work, then she would slip poison into his wine. His behaviour would thus determine her course of action: the onus was on him.

'I have come to see the ship,' she said, 'and petition that I join it.'

'Change ships?' said Reners, visibly impacted by the very idea. 'I cannot have you jump ship on a whim. No, seriously, Madame Stuart, I sincerely regret the incident last night. I really don't know what came over me.' But May stood wordless, staring over the balustrade, the wind in her fiery hair.

'I mean, I will certainly make it worth your while . . .' persisted Reners in an effort to recapture her attention.

'How strange,' returned May, still gazing out to sea.

'On the contrary,' said the captain, 'it's only natural that a lady of your standing should receive a handsome reward.'

May ignored his words. Instead, she looked out to sea and said: 'Why are they raising the English flag, do you think?'

'I beg your pardon,' said Reners, now turning his head to follow her gaze toward the approaching ship. 'Good God!' said Reners, who stood stone still for a moment before the realisation sank in. 'I believe we are about to be attacked.'

'Can't you outrun it?'

'She's a sloop, Madame,' said Reners irritably, implying it would be impossible to outrun such a ship.

'Well, you're not going to just stand here and wait for us to be fleeced, are you?'

'If we were closer to nightfall, we might have lost her, but we are not. There's a whole day ahead of us. There is no way we can outrun her.'

May suddenly imagined her possessions being carried away by grubby privateers. She said: 'But I have my effects, Captain.'

'Then I suggest you go to your cabin and lock your bloody door, Madame! Or it won't be just your jewels they'll be taking!'

*

Captain Reners was a merchant, a popinjay, and a profiteer. He was not a soldier.

As soon as he saw the English flag hoisted instead of the French ensign, he knew what he was in for. Only privateers would employ such dastardly tactics in order to get in close to a merchantman with the intention to board. In all his seafaring career, he had only been accosted by sea rovers twice, but each time, the merchandise did not personally belong to him. Yet there was nothing he could have done even if they had displayed their colours three cables out, he said to himself in an effort to get over the shock and give his mind space to think up a plan. He passed through it the strategies open to him and quickly singled out one that would save his precious chattel. He would have to cut his losses and forego his barrelled goods. The barrelled goods belonged to merchants. If indeed they were privateers sailing under an English flag, then they would probably have no desire to deal with Negroes, reasoned Reners. For they would attract the wrath of every government and become the prey of every nation's navy. It was becoming clear that Africans were becoming the muscle and might to tame these savage lands. So Reners resolved to try to save his precious slaves, even if it meant throwing the lady into the bargain. In the eyes of your common villain, she would make a handsome ransom, and by the time the truth become known, he and his shipload would be high and dry.

*

Didier Ducamp, standing by Captain Brook, knew that in this game, you sometimes had to just weather the storm till you hit more clement skies.

For every run of good fortune inevitably led to a mishap. You just had to take it on the chin when it came and get over it as quickly as you could. And nine times out of ten, the next prize would be a breeze. But the previous run-in had knocked the stuffing out of him. So when he saw the French merchantman strike her colours, he sensed a wave of relief and jubilation spreading through the ship's very fibre as the mates let out hoots and clanked their sabres and cutlasses against the gunwale timbers.

The sloop swept past the merchantman on the leeside, then manoeuvred around the French ship's aft to lay up beside her on the larboard.

*

Shocked and horrified, May Stuart observed the manoeuvre from her window.

As she fastened her two pockets around her waist under her petticoat and placed a pocket pistol in one of them, she reflected on how quickly the winds of fortune could change. How quickly a self-made woman could lose all her fortune and tumble back into poverty when there was no one to cushion the fall. Only yesterday, she was a very important passenger, none other than the niece of the governor of Saint-Domingue, travelling on urgent business to the English settlement to fetch her daughter before hostilities between France and England escalated into war. 'Pig's breath!' she said between gritted teeth, resisting the temptation to cry, her hands now on her smooth forehead. God, it was so unfair.

*

The sloop trimmed her sails. 'Ahoy!' called out Reners in French from the quarterdeck bulwark as the adversary came to the merchantman's starboard aft. 'Where are ye bound?'

Leaning over the sloop gunwale, Captain Brook hollered: 'Aboard your ship!' Behind Brook, cannon muzzles showed through the portside bulwark, and there was a man posted behind every swivel gun along the gunwale. The rest of the crew now lowered their voices to let their captain find out what was what. 'Surrender, Captain, surrender in good faith, or on our next round, blood will be dripping plentiful through ye decks like a stuck sow! Let us board, and you have my promise you will be well used.' Brook then arched his back as a chorus of roars and threats belted out from the horde of terrifying seamen.

It was pointless, Reners pretending he had an option, Reners thought to himself, outnumbered as they were five to one. The merchantman crew had primed the cannons, all six of them as the sloop had approached, but Reners knew they would be no match. They would all be slaughtered, and this pirate captain looked like a damnable fellow if ever there was. No, his only chance was to sit the enemy around a negotiating table, where he knew he had the capacity to talk his way out of a devil's lair with any man in the Caribbean, even in English. He knew too well how to flatter the mind of a desperado. Twenty years of cruising the Caribbean, and Reners knew every type of haunt where a man could forget his woes and lose his morals. He knew how their minds worked, that they favoured speed, did not tolerate hanging about. Give them what they wanted as quick as you could, and they would be itching to be on their way. So he thought.

*

While some of the crew climbed to the yards to stow away the sails and immobilize the vessel, Ducamp led a dozen rovers to round up any laggers below deck.

She was a good size, solidly built, and offered double the storage space of the sloop. He could soon see that the deck was partitioned off. And a glance into her hold told him it would have taken a good few hours to offload the best of the cargo onto the sloop.

'Alleluia!' exclaimed Billy Hawke, 'they've still got chickens!' The birds were strutting about the dim deck, and Ducamp soon saw why. Their usual habitat in the partitioned segment at the forepart had been given over to slaves. He pushed open the door and could do nothing better than stare at the wretches. Some of them stared back, wide-eyed, with both fear and hope in their eyes. Perhaps they perceived something of sympathy and kindness in the looks of this stranger, and, feeling instinctively that their liberation might have come, began to shout and reach out their hands held back by irons and chains.

'More of 'em over here,' said Billy Hawke. 'Bloody stinks to high heaven!'

Ducamp strode back down the deck to an iron latticed door where a few dark, lame faces tried to crane their necks, their eyes lit up, to see what was going on. But most of them remained with their heads resting on sackcloth, as if they were too dejected or too weak to raise them, though their eyes expressed a kind of solemn contentment. Ducamp had to look away a moment; he had seen slaves on a plantation but had never seen them in transit. Some of the frail creatures looked barely older than children, a few scrambling up on their knees, stretching out their hands, others content to watch listlessly.

'Fetch the keys and bring 'em out on deck,' said Ducamp with solemnity, 'so the able-bodied can look after the lame.' Then he turned to one of the ship's sailors and grabbed him by the shirt. He said: 'Any more surprises like this?'

The stocky man with a large head and small, crafty eyes had a tranquil air about him, as if he had nothing to fear. He said calmly: 'Just the two cabins, mate, forty-eight slaves last count.' Ducamp let the man go, for this man as well as the other half-dozen crew members could well end up as shipmates if they chose to, and this one looked as if he knew it. 'But there be a fine lady at the stern,' added the sailor, whose name Ducamp would come to know as Mattis. He gave a lascivious curl of the lip. Billy, standing aside, widened his eyes at the thought of a woman aboard and passed his hand over his dry lips.

'Where at the stern?' growled Ducamp, irritably.

'Special cabin, starboard,' replied Mattis, with a knowing grin. The wily sailor knew as well as the next man you should never take sides until the cards were dealt. It was wiser to leave all your options open . . .

Ducamp raised his thick arm and wiped his nose on the top of his armpit to fill his nostrils with his own scent, and chase away the foul stench of African piss, sweat, and sick. 'Billy, Mossa, once you've got the poor bastards out, line 'em up and bring 'em up for air,' he ordered. Turning to another mate, he said: 'Fimbar, you go check what we got in the hold.' Leaving the men with their orders, Ducamp strode to the aft at a brisk pace, for he had noticed more than one lust-hungry glare on the mention of a woman aboard.

*

May heard harried footsteps as the crew were herded above deck, and then gruff voices through the floorboards of the captain's cabin directly above hers.

To stay calm, she had kept herself busy silently stashing away her effects, and had locked her large trunk. Now she stood, ears pricked to the ambient sounds of sailors swarming the ship. Judging by their growled commands and boisterous laughs of victory, it became clear to her that these men were not from the navy. They were privateers, and more often than not, privateers were harsh, grabbing, lowly bred villains of the sea who lacked the finesse of the trained officer. Even in her former life, she had steered clear of them.

Should she show herself, or should she hide? she wondered, her heart thumping nineteen to the dozen. But where would she hide? As she stood weighing up the dilemma, heavy footsteps approaching relieved her from making a decision. She pulled out a pistol from her pocket under her dress and turned to face the door being rattled from the other side.

'Ouvrez la porte!' said Ducamp, who imagined this lady must be French. 'Open the door, or I'll kick it open!'

'I am armed,' returned the female voice in stern, accented French on the other side of the door, her statement punctuated by the sound of a gun being cocked.

Tricky, thought Ducamp, but there was nonetheless a timber door between him and the holder of the gun. Without giving the lady time to think, he stepped back and crashed a boot through the door panel. Then he passed a

48

hand inside, groped to push up the latch bar, and he burst into the room.

'Stop right there. Any further and I'll shoot you!' said May, facing the big, grubby man standing in the doorframe, his hair black with pitch. She took aim, knowing that if she missed his heart, he would just reach out and grab her. She steeled herself and looked into the eyes that peered down from a rugged, symmetrical face, one whose furrowed brow was not that of an angry man, but condescending and interrogating. Then he spoke.

'Shoot, and you'll be pulled to pieces like carrion, after being passed around like a bottle o' rum,' said Ducamp, who now looked into the large green-and-gold-speckled eyes that glared back at him in defiance and fear. He held her gaze and studied her stance, her simple but refined appearance, and her shock of auburn hair bundled on top of her head. Still locking eyes with hers, he took a slow step forward. He said softly: 'Put the gun down, and I promise no one will hurt you.'

His voice was calm, hardly louder than a whisper, like a distant rumble of rolling thunder, yet still deep and powerful enough to send vibrations down her throat. 'Stop, I say,' she said, trying to make her voice commanding, but she could not help feeling it was a feeble sound compared to the man's deep resonance.

Didier took another slow step forward, holding her stare, to anticipate her next move. But her large eyes were drawing him in; her full-lipped mouth made him want to kiss her and was making him lose focus. 'Look, lady, put it down, and you'll be all right.'

In a more commanding voice, she said: 'Then promise you won't touch me . . . or my effects!' May knew a pirate's

49

promise was not worth the saliva spat out with it, but she needed a pretext to save face.

'Can't speak for the crew, but I personally promise you'll not be harmed if you put the gun down and come with me.'

Suddenly, hurried footsteps in the corridor made her edgy and pleated her smooth forehead. Ducamp knew the fright could cause her to pull the trigger. He lunged forward, and covered the small muff pistol and her hand with his large paw. In the same movement, he snatched the gun away, dashed it onto the bunk, and then held her arms.

'Let me go, you brute!' she blurted out, furious.

'I won't hurt you,' he said, holding her tense exquisitely soft body.

Overpowered by both his brute force and his male scent, May, seeing that he made no attempt to grab any part of her anatomy other than her arms, which he pinned to her side, stamped her foot and stood still. 'All right, let me go then!' she said. He did as he was told, but then grabbed her by the wrist and pulled her along.

'But you're coming with me,' he said. 'It's for your own good, believe me, lady!'

'Let go, I do not require to be led like a wild beast,' said May proudly. She slipped her hand through his fingers. Then she led the way to the upper deck past Johnny Reed rubbing his whiskers.

A few minutes later, May walked into the captain's cabin, followed by Ducamp, as Reners was saying: 'I insist, you cannot take anything under the English flag, Sir, so what is the meaning of this intrusion?'

Captain Brook, leaning on the chart table, turned to acknowledge Ducamp, and ignoring the woman, he said: 'Speaks good English, don't he, Ducamp, eh?' Then turning slowly back to Reners seated behind the table, he said: 'Well, Cap'n, this intrusion, as you put it, is our way of life. Get me drift?'

'But you would be in breach of international law, Sir. Why, it would equate to no less than an act of piracy!'

May thought the captain had more courage than she had credited him with. But she wished he would not push it too far, for clearly, these villains were not concerned with international law, or any law for that matter.

Brook looked at the merchant captain, then to Ducamp. Then he gave a little chuckle of false amusement and said to Captain Reners: 'Well, you'd better wipe your French arse with that, then!' Brook had pulled out the letter of marque from his pocket and held it up close to the French captain's face. 'Our two nations are at war, Captain!'

'Oh,' said Reners, caught off guard. 'I see.' He looked around vacantly while searching in his mind for a bargaining handle.

'So you see, Cap'n, since we've overrun your ship, your little business now belongs to us, and their majesties. But let's have a gander and see what you got to offer, shall we?'

'I'll tell you . . . I have black slaves and barrelled goods: cocoa, sugar, ginger, and some annatto . . .'

'Now you're talking. We'll take the blacks,' said Brook, to the surprise of Reners. Didier was not surprised; he knew Brook's tactic of preaching false intentions to get to the truth. Brook continued. 'In good condition, are they?'

'No, actually, they are not. I have had to segregate the sick, already lost four of them. You wouldn't be wanting to be taking them, Captain.'

'All right, then, what you got for me in exchange?' said Brook, sitting on the table and looking the merchant captain in the eye. Ducamp could see he was enjoying the little charade, and that the merchant captain did not know how to fathom the curl on Brook's lip. Even Ducamp failed more often than not to read whether it was complaisantly sincere or pleated in derision. Probably Brook himself was between the two moods. Was he talking in jest, or just being sardonic? 'Out with it then,' he said. 'You, the vanquished, tell me, the vanquisher, what I should take, or shall I tell you? But I'll tell you what: let's start with gold . . .'

'I don't deal in gold, Captain.'

'I'm sure you must have some stashed away on such a fine ship. Tell you what: you tell me where you keep it, and I'll let you keep your Negroes. How's that sound, Captain?'

'I am not carrying gold or treasure, Sir, I can assure you. But . . .' Reners passed his hand over his chin and rubbed his sweaty throat. At last, with a fleeting glance at his very important passenger, he said: 'But, as a bonus for leaving me the slaves, I would be prepared to leave you the lady, a fine lady too . . .'

May felt an irrepressible surge of indignation rise in her bosom. Her eyes fired a shot at Reners.

'Women and ships don't match in my book, mate!' said Brook.

Reners said: 'Ah, but this one's special—'

Now pulling out the knife in her pocket, May lunged forward. 'You scoundrel, you filthy swine! Don't you dare!' she hurled. She would not be sold like a filthy street whore to these men or any man. She would rather kill him than hear him tell of her past. If these rogues found out about it, she would be passed around like a whiskey bottle just like the big sailor had suggested, and be lucky to escape with her life.

Luckily for Reners, Ducamp caught her hand holding the dagger and swung her round. 'Don't you dare, or I swear to God I will kill you! I will kill you!' shouted May as she struggled to get free from the strong arms of her captor.

'Drop the knife!' said Ducamp. May calmed for an instant, just enough time for Ducamp to relax his hold slightly. Then she kneed him smartly in the nuts, and continued her course toward Reners as Ducamp clasped her elbow again and swung her round. In the rage and momentum of the moment, she jabbed him under the left arm before he could immobilize the offending hand by holding back her forearm.

'Let up, woman!' roared Brook, pointing a flintlock at her, 'or I'll end your woes here and now!' May dropped the knife; she slumped under the nervous tension and let Ducamp dump her unceremoniously into a chair.

'All right, man?' said Brook to the bosun.

'It's nothing,' said Didier, pressing a hand to his side. His pitch-dowsed jerkin, which he had recently acquired, showed nothing of the wound.

'Hah,' cried Brook, 'nicked by a lass!' Then he holstered his musket in his baldric with its brothers and turned back to the matter in hand.

'As I was about to say,' continued Reners, who had retained his composure, 'this spirited young lady is worth her weight in gold. For she is none other than the niece of the governor of Saint-Domingue.'

'So?' said Brook.

May wanted to shout out, but she held her tongue; at least this way, she was still a fine lady in the eyes of those present. The scoundrel, though, she thought to herself, had deliberately opted to reveal her as a governor's niece rather than as a courtesan because it offered him greater bargaining power, as if she were a commodity. But she could hardly declare herself to be otherwise.

Reners continued. 'Governor de Cussy is a rich man, Captain. He has interests in salvage; he will pay a good price, I am sure. Leave me the Negroes, and take the barrelled goods and Madame Stuart.'

'This true?' said Brook, looking around to May.

'Yes…' she said with a snarl of assent; then she pursed her lips before anything else came out.

'Hmm,' said Brook, turning to Ducamp. 'Don't care to have a woman aboard my ship. Don't see the point in 'em, but this one might get us into Port-de-Paix . . . And I know an English navy commander who'll be mighty pleased with the catch, and we make double the money, savvy?' Turning back to the merchant captain, he said: 'All right, you got a deal.'

Ducamp was not duped by Brook's quick assent. He already knew Brook's intentions and the real deal.

'I am glad I could accommodate you, Captain,' said Reners, flitting his eyes nervously between Ducamp and Brook in case the former raised an issue. But Ducamp said nothing. 'So that is agreed, then. Slaves will only encumber you. You will leave them with me, and you will take the barrels, and the fine lady.'

'Aye, and a fine ship you have here, Cap'n, mighty fine, my compliments. She didn't look much from afar, but now I'm inside of her, I believe she be a fine ship,' said Brook, planting a hand on Reners's shoulder as the latter got up from the chair.

'Made to last, of cedar no less . . .' said Reners, while May watched him, cat-eyed.

'Makes a difference, see, Ducamp,' said Brook, turning

to the bosun, 'especially when soaked in the briny sea for any length of time. Don't need so much careening.' He turned back to Reners. 'Mine's made of oak,' he pursued, 'waterlogged oak, I oughta say. Needs careening, but she handles well when her hull's free of pesky barnacles and seagrass. Wouldn't be surprised if yourn outran mine, by thunder, seeing as she is right now!'

It suddenly occurred to Reners that if he had made a run for it, he might have saved his barrels, and retained the company of Madame Stuart. He could have sworn she flashed him a smug grin. Brook continued: 'Aye, heavy with the sea inside of her, and about as lithe as a dull stream, hardly a ship for a Brook, hah!' Decidedly, the captain was in good spirits, thought Didier, who gave a chuckle, knowing he was up to something.

Brook led the way out of the captain's quarters onto the quarterdeck. Then he strode to the balustrade to address the captured men standing subdued below him. He saw moments like these as a prime opportunity to recruit able seamen for a stint or an entire cruise, and he always enjoyed venting his drafting patter to induce the men to sign the articles.

'Mates,' he said, his back arched upright with his two hands holding the rail, 'always beats me when good seamen risk their lives for a pauper's pay. But if you join us, we won't belittle you with a pitiful wage. We wouldn't stoop so low, because any mate of ours gets a one-part share of booty, and if you're looking for a position, there's a surgeon's and a carpenter's job up for grabs if there's any of you with experience in those lines. So I put it to you, lads. Come with us, or go with them . . .'

Reners was barely able to contain his outrage. 'Captain,'

he said, stepping into Brook's field of vision on his left side. 'Captain, we said nothing of taking my crew. How will I navigate?'

'Oh, don't worry, man. I've already thought of that,' said Brook, tapping Captain Reners on the lapel. He then motioned to his men to bring the slaves out. They were unchained, dazed by the sunlight, some of them propping up their sick fellows. Ducamp deduced that one of the boys must have slipped a word in Brook's ear when the bosun was below deck with the lady. Reners looked on, incredulous and with a bad feeling. 'Monbossa,' called Brook. He called every black chief whose name he did not know by his version of "my boss" in a pseudo African language. The leading slave, with an authoritative bearing, looked up at the captain as he stood on the quarterdeck. 'Get yourselves aboard that ship, mates,' continued Brook, pointing to the two gangplanks secured between the ships to enable a passage back and forth.

It was an unsteady crossing for sure—one usually made for rolling barrels from ship to ship—and it was one the blacks guardedly embraced. Were they really being offered a way to freedom?

'And take my advice, if you come upon any live meat, better keep it fresh and lively till it's time for the chop, eh, Mombossa?' The black stared back at Brook to gauge his sincerity, then gave a half nod and continued toward the gangplanks.

'Captain, I thought we had a deal!' interrupted Reners, sternly.

'And so we do, and I'm a man of my word, Sir.'

'Then why are you taking my slaves?'

'Oh, I ain't taking your slaves,' said Brook. 'See, don't sit well with me seeing men chained up. No, Cap'n Reners, I'm taking your ship!' Brook then turned back to the captured crew and said: 'Now, lads, it's up to you . . . Would you rather live a life on a straw bed, drinking watered-down wine and seeing your wench work her fingers to the bone? Would you rather bow so low you end up walking with a stoop? Would you?' There came boos from the privateers guarding the captives. Brook continued: 'Or would you rather spread your limbs between silk sheets, put spice on your beef, and make merry with mates and ladies so sweet you just wanna shower 'em with ruby kisses and pearls?'

'Aye!' came the chorus. This time, the captives joined in while Ducamp paraphrased in French.

'But it's up to you, me hearties. It's your liberty to take or leave. But beware, you won't never get another chance! So I put it to you, lads. You stayin' 'ere for a cruise or three with ole Cap'n Brook and his hearty band? Or you goin' over there?' Brook pointed to the sloop that the freed blacks were boarding on one side, and where barrels and possessions were being brought across on the other.

While a storm tossed and turned in Reners's belly, his men took a moment to glance at each other. Then, in unison, they let out a hearty cheer. Even Mattis, Reners's main mate, was averse to joining the freed slaves aboard the sloop.

Reners stood scandalised and fretful as it dawned on him that not only were these rogues about to steal his ship, they were about to set him on a ship full of unchained slaves, his slaves. 'Sir,' he let out, trying to maintain some dignity despite the turmoil inside, 'Sir, this is an act of piracy—'

'It would be if we weren't at war,' returned Brook quite merrily. Turning to the two mates who had just lugged the captain's trunk onto the quarterdeck, with a sardonic grin,

57

he said: 'Conduct the captain to his new ship, lads . . . hah!' To Captain Reners, he said: 'Fear not, Cap'n. Play it right, and you'll be all right. They'll need someone to navigate. You get me drift?'

But Captain Reners suddenly saw visions of himself being skinned alive. In a desperate bid to save his life, he stepped out and seized Madame Stuart, who had followed everyone out of the cabin. Holding a pistol to her pretty temple, he said: 'I will kill her, and it will be your fault. The governor will send a party for your head.' Now he had to think quick, and he had to keep his demand within the realm of the acceptable for the privateer. He said: 'Put the slaves in chains, and I'll board, or I'll kill her now. And I don't care if you shoot me after.'

Brook gave a smile of condescension. How would anyone know who killed who out in the middle of the sea? The other privateers present looked on, more peeved than panicked.

Only Ducamp showed any defensive reaction, as if his previous exchange with May obliged him to rally to her defence. 'Wait!' he said, addressing Reners in French. 'Nice and slowly, Captain, and we can make a deal.' He turned to Brook. 'Can't we, Cap'n!'

Brook slowly moved his head from side to side. 'Pwah, a lot o' messing for a bit o' strumpet, ain't it, though?'

'A governor's niece,' corrected Ducamp in May's defence.

'All righty, let her go, and we'll chain the niggers. That what you want?'

'Chain them, and place them in the hold.'

'All right, but let her go first, man.'

'Do I have your word as a fellow captain and man of the sea?'

58

'I give you my oath,' grunted Brook. 'Now, let the fine lady go. She's my pot of gold, remember?'

Reners hardly had a choice. He lowered his pistol while Ducamp pulled May away from harm's reach. As he did so, he instinctively placed his free hand on his knife wound that now gave him pain as he reached for the lady. He noticed that jerkin showed a damp patch where he had been stabbed and that the bottom of his undershirt was soaked. But his attention was diverted to the sinister scene playing out in front of him.

'Right,' growled Brook to the two bearers. 'Now march him over the bloody plank!'

Reners, stunned and incredulous, said: 'You gave me your word, Captain!'

'You take the word of a man who has just stolen your ship? Ha, ha, ha, shame on you, Captain!'

'They'll slaughter him,' said Ducamp.

'Not if they wanna get somewhere,' said Brook, tapping the side of his head in connivance.

'They'll kill him once they get where they want.'

'Then he'll have to talk sharp, won't he. It's a man-eat-man world out here, bosun. You know that.'

May Stuart watched Captain Reners, the marriageable gentleman, the lusty commander, and the nasty slaver, as he was frogmarched away. He turned and held her stare as he was pushed onto the gangplank. Raising a finger at her he hurled out: 'Ha, but she's a whore! She's a bloody whore!' But the danger had passed, at least for May, for no one listened to him as he struggled against the thick, burly arms that were now virtually carrying him over the planks to his fate. He became increasingly unnerved. 'Wait,' he shouted desperately. 'No, wait, I'd rather you shoot me. Shoot me, I beg you!' he hurled out as the blacks gathered around the other end of the gangplank to meet him in the sloop.

'Nah, you'll be all right,' called Brook, quite amused at the captain's change of tone. 'If they wanna navigate her, they'll have to keep you alive. Then you can get to know them better. Get me drift?'

The merchant captain was pushed onto the aptly named *Joseph*, the ship that by some twist of fate bore his name. What happened next defied Brook's expectations, and filled May with lasting horror.

Once the sailors had shoved Reners over the bulwark and into the ship, and he found himself slowly encircled by dark, vengeful faces. 'Stop them!' May cried out in anticipation of an appalling prospect.

'Bah, they're just putting the fear of the devil in him, Ladyship. They'll be needing a navigator . . .' said Brook, who could not take his eyes off the dark crowd as it thickened around Joseph Reners. The French captain now let out a cry of panic as he brandished his loaded pistol. But he only had one shot, so he turned it against himself. As he did so, the silent, angry crowd let out a collective cry and lunged forward like a pack of hounds. Amid terrible screams, his clothes were torn from his person and flung into the air as he became engulfed in a mad scramble of clawed and fisted hands, and a shimmering knife—his knife. Then came bits of flesh and his genitals, followed by his fingers, then his limbs.

'Oh,' said a fascinated Brook when the dreadful cries had ceased, 'apparently, they didn't need a navigator after all. Didn't think of that!'

Ducamp turned away, stunned and appalled at the savage execution. But appalled, too, at the acts that must have driven those men to tear another human being apart limb by limb.

Uncovering her eyes, May turned to the only privateer who had shown any sympathy when she was seized, and she allowed him to escort her to her cabin. She was in for a rough voyage, she told herself; she was going to have to show her true grit. For what would happen when these men inevitably found out from the governor of Saint-Domingue that she was not his niece? What would they do when they discovered she was nothing more than a bit of strumpet as the pirate captain had suggested, albeit in jest?

SIX

MAY SAT AT her cabin table.

Moving with the pitch of the ship, she endeavoured to thread a line of waxed silk through the eye of a needle.

There was only one way to turn the ship around, she thought to herself, but she had to act quickly. For if Brook found out she was an impostor, her fine person would not be worth two cassava cakes, let alone its weight in gold. She had already seen what he was capable of, and the mere thought of the dreadful fate of Captain Reners made her shudder. Yes, she had a plan, but she would need an ally to put it into action; otherwise, she would give herself away, and nobody would want to be thought of as a courtesan on a ship full of pirates. Because for all their talk of fighting under the English banner and their letter of marque, that was clearly what they were, pirates. Pirates under the guise of privateers, and she had just the thing for pirates.

A knock at the door interrupted her train of thought. 'Who goes there?' she called out guardedly.

'Ducamp . . . Me Lady.' Didier disliked addressing the so-called wellborn according to the received etiquette. Ever since he had removed himself from social convention, he could see more clearly that it was designed to make them feel superior because it put them on a pedestal. There again, he disliked being thought of as uncouth, so his announcement sounded awkward in his mouth.

'Vous pouvez entrer, Monsieur Ducamp,' said May. 'As long as you do not put your foot through the door again!'

He pushed the door to find the fine lady delicately perched on the edge of her stool before her table, upon which sat a medicine chest. She had been allowed to keep her quarters in return for tending to Joe, the captain's sick mulatto.

Captain Brook normally loathed womenfolk, whom he considered poison, especially onboard a ship. But he recognised that they had their utility when it came to caring for the sick and wounded, if naught else. What was more, the lady had a medicine chest from which she had given Joe some laudanum so that he could sleep soundly for once, and to Brook, she would be worth all the wenches in the world if she could put the lad on his feet again.

'I have some laudanum,' she said, swivelling round and flashing her eyes into Ducamp's.

'Won't be necessary, just a scratch,' he said, softly closing the door which had been patched up with a plank where his foot had crashed through it.

'As you wish. Please take a seat.' She indicated for him to sit on the bunk past the window. 'It will hurt,' she said, swabbing a cloth with alcohol. 'But first, I must cleanse the wound . . . And you shall need to remove your shirt. Oh, you needn't be coy, Monsieur, I am a widow, and I have treated men's wounds before.'

Ducamp gave a grunt of assent and removed his bloodstained shirt to reveal a powerful torso and muscular

63

arms flecked with battle scars. The smell of the male invaded her senses as she approached him. Then she touched his bare skin with her free hand and began dabbing the open wound with the other, working from the outside. He tensed a little while he got used to the sting. Then he watched her attentive face, her unblinking eyes transfixed on the wound, her silky coppery hair tied back in a chignon on top of her head, and her smooth forehead pleated in thought.

'I did not mean to harm you, Monsieur Ducamp,' she said, sensing his eyes upon her. 'But the next time you come at me with those thumping great hands of yours, I swear to God I will kill you!' She pressed the cloth full over the centre of the wound and glanced up with a straight smile as he tensed again.

'Hah, will you now,' he let out with an indulgent chuckle at her sense of vengeance. 'Not if I kill you first!'

She pressed the wound again; he tensed. 'Hurt?' she said. 'No.'

'Good. I shall have to stitch it.'

'It's just a cut.'

'But it's cut crosswise: the lips will not hold together with a bandage. It would have been better if I had stabbed you lengthwise; they would have closed naturally together with the aid of a tight bandage. I shall give you the stick to bite on, as you refused the laudanum,' she said with a superior smile.

'I didn't know ladies gave themselves to surgery.'

'You judge quickly, Monsieur. Now, do you want me to close the wound, or would you rather it become infected?'

Rolling his eyes, he gave another grunt of assent. She swung round to pick up the stitching needle, a cannula from the chest, and a piece of soft wood for him to sink his teeth into.

'May I ask, Monsieur Ducamp,' she said, holding the block of wood at the ready, 'what makes you side with the enemy? I mean, you are French, are you not?'

Didier arched his back, tensing for a different reason this time. Slightly irate, he said: 'I've done my time fighting the king's wars for a lieutenant's wage. Now I fight for yours truly.' He slammed his large right palm onto his firm bosom, which made a dull thud.

May secretly noted he had not been a simple soldier; he had acquired rank, which in May's eyes gave him status. 'But doesn't it make you feel like a . . . a traitor?' she insisted in false naiveté, which, since she had embarked on her first tour of service, had become second nature to her.

Didier was nobody's fool; he could tell when a woman was trying to draw him out. The charade irritated him nonetheless. 'I don't belong to France, no more than I belong to the French king!' he said indignantly. 'Like I said, I've done my time fighting wars for a pittance just to fill the coffers of noblemen—noblemen like the one who didn't even have the decency to give folk of my village dead from the flux a proper grave! Nay, I'm my own man now. I fight for my own skin; that's all.' He held her searching gaze for a moment.

Seeing she had struck a raw nerve, she returned a straight-lipped smile that gave nothing away, although deep down, she sensed she might have found her ally.

Didier was unused to being put on the back foot and, breaking the short silence that ensued, he said: 'And what's an English lady doing fraternising with the French?'

'The English killed my husband,' said May, and then promptly inserted the stick between Ducamp's teeth.

Next, she placed the cannula, a slender silver pipe with an

eye at the end, against the inside lip of the gash. Its purpose was to hold the wound firmly while the needle was being pushed through. With her right hand, she thrust her needle into the skin and pushed it through until it appeared in the previously positioned eye of the cannula. She repeated the operation, only this time placing the cannula on the skin on the opposite lip where the needle would poke through, thus enabling her to end up with two ends of the thread so she could tie the suture. Ducamp bit hard into the block of wood. He wanted to cry out to evacuate the pain, but he kept it in. May continued diligently threading and closing the wound with each suture as she spoke. In spite of being in the throes of pain, Ducamp quickly realised that she had done this before, which was surprising for a lady of high birth, wasn't it?

'They used him as a privateer, then hanged him for piracy,' she said, after she'd tied another suture. 'On his death, I took to residing in Havana, where I picked up intelligence which I sold to the French. Then I took intelligence from the French and the English and sold it to the Spanish. I would hop from Saint Pierre to Port Royale, then to Havana and Port-de-Paix, staying in each port a few months at a time.' She took another pre-threaded needle from the needle case, which gave Ducamp a respite. Then she pushed it through the lip of the wound as before, to make another suture. Didier locked his teeth onto the block of wood, tensing every muscle in his jaw. 'So you see, Lieutenant Ducamp,' she said, pulling the needle out the other side as if she were stitching a lady's hem, 'we are not so very different, you and I, for I have also been on the account.' Ducamp winced as the needle was driven into his skin again to the opposite lip and in through the eye of the silver cannula.

May had not intended to give so much away all at once.

But she felt liberated to get it off her chest, and for some reason beyond the scope of logic, she felt she could trust this man, this privateer cum pirate, a trained killer of men, who had nonetheless saved her from being shot for the price of a knife wound, caused by her. As with many taciturn menfolk who looked stern and powerful, she detected within him a sense of honour and justice, and that he would not be such a tough nut to crack. It seemed fitting to her now that she had already gotten under his skin. But most of all, it was her only chance, and judging people's character in this New World—a world where people moved on so quickly—was critical to anyone's survival, let alone their success. 'Try to keep still, Lieutenant. You are doing very well; we are nearly there,' she said more gently, flashing her large green-and-gold eyes at him. She continued with her stitching and her story. 'So you see, I am not the governor's niece, you have been cheated, and I am left in quite a predicament.'

He winced.

She continued. 'For your captain is going to be very upset to find that Governor de Cussy will not give a silver dollar for my welfare, never mind my weight in gold . . . There,' she said, once she had tied the last suture. Then she removed the stick from Ducamp's mouth.

Raising his left arm, he looked down to inspect the wound, then levelled his eyes at May. 'So you're not a fine English lady, then.'

'That is not what I said, Lieutenant,' said May, defiantly holding his regard. 'Moreover, it is my belief that whether or not I am a fine lady lies in the eye of the beholder.' He looked down again at his wound.

'Well, Madame,' he said, 'you certainly have a seamstress's touch.'

May did not find the remark very funny. With a mirthless smile, she proceeded in covering the wound with a lint pledget, smeared with ointment, and a compress before reaching for a long roll of linen.

'I seem to have put your nose out,' said Ducamp.

'Rest assured, you have not,' she returned, passing the roll around his torso. 'But like I said, we are not dissimilar, you and I. We are both running for ourselves. Except that I already have my treasure and, before you so rudely interrupted our course, was returning north to recover the greater part of it and settle down.'

By now, Ducamp was reaching the limit of his word intake. He said: 'You have my sympathies, Madame, but why are you telling me this?'

'Because if it's silver you are after, then I have a plan that may get you some. Lots.'

'Go on,' said Ducamp, suddenly more relaxed now that the body's natural painkiller was throbbing through his veins. Her fine hair tickled softly as it brushed against his bare chest, her delicate perfume inebriating him, and the closeness of her body was making him feel aroused. It had been a long time since a pretty woman had tended to him, and it was all he could do to prevent his prick from stiffening. At that instant, as she held his torso between her hands, he was faintly aware that she could use him like a puppet.

'Well,' she continued, lowering her voice to a confidential tone while straightening his torso and adjusting the linen band. 'I gave the governor information about Spanish plans to join forces with the English to invade Saint Kitts. I also found out about a salvage operation off the coast of Florida. Silver bars recovered from a sunken payroll ship.

The silver has been deposited at a Spanish settlement and awaits recovery by a Spanish fleet. At least, that is what the letter says.'

'Letter?'

'Yes, it fell from an officer's pocket when I was in Havana. I can show it to you once you agree to my deal. It says that a fleet will be sent shortly once they have assembled enough ships.'

An image flashed into Ducamp's mind of the sunken ship, and he suddenly became alert and attentive, sobered despite her persistent perfume. 'Go on,' he said.

She continued. 'But I happened to know that the ships were destined for an attack on the French territory in case of war. And according to your captain, war there is!'

'Which means the recovery will be delayed.'

'That is what the letter was about.'

'And you want me to tell the captain?'

'Yes.'

'Why can't you?'

'Because I would lose my commercial value. I cannot be thought of as anything other than the governor's niece, and what would a governor's niece be doing with such a letter, other than having come across it in all innocence by accident?'

'A bit far-fetched!'

'Well it's all we've got. You know as well as I do what it would mean if I lost my value aboard a ship full of broody pirates.'

'Privateers.'

'Privateers, pirates, makes no difference.'

'Aye, I s'pose you're not wrong there. And your deal?'

'I need you to find a reason to go to Charles Town. Say, to refit the ship. Once there, I can take care of myself,' she said, tying a final knot of the linen band. 'There, all done! Now, do we have a deal?'

*

Half an hour later, Ducamp showed May into the captain's cabin, where Brook was bearing down on the ship's navigation chart.

On top of it, May saw the Spanish missive she had given to Ducamp a little earlier. Captain Ned Brook looked up, and in feigned etiquette, he said: 'This yours, Your Ladyship?' He held up the Spanish letter.

'No,' said May brazenly, showing an equal lack of ceremony.

'Whose is it, then?'

'It belonged to my uncle.'

'Oh, you mean the governor of Saint-Domingue,' he returned, with incredulity in his voice.

'Yes. I must have taken it by accident when he gave me my travel document. Is it important?'

'Important? Hah, too bloody right it's important. It's from Havana, but what I wanna know is, how did a French governor get his hands on a top-secret Spanish missive?'

'Why, I suspect he has his informants, Captain,' said May, as if it were obvious.

'Oh, right, why didn't I think of that?' said Brook, raising a sardonic eyebrow, the curl on his lip caught between derision and amusement. 'So he has his informants, has he?'

'I suppose so.'

'And I suppose you wouldn't be one of 'em, would ya, Your Ladyship?' Brook stared at the woman with slight distaste. He did not like women much at the best of times, and this one was particularly striking with her flaming hair and large green eyes.

'I beg your pardon?' returned May, feigning surprise and indignation.

'Somink don't rhyme, see. I mean, for starters, what's an English lady doing with a French uncle?'

'The governor is my uncle *par alliance*,' said May.

'And what's an English lady doing married to a Frenchman, then?'

'Our two countries were not at war when we wed, neither were they when he died,' said May with solemnity. 'The governor had kindly allowed me to travel back to Charles Town to be with my family. That is where we were headed when you intercepted us.'

'What was your husband's name, then?'

'Why, Stuart.'

'You mean, Stuart, like King bloody James Stuart?'

'No, Captain. Stuart, as in Monsieur Stuart de Cussy,' she said, pronouncing the name in highbrow French. She guessed that Brook ignored the finer subtleties of the French language. Ducamp, on the other hand, would find the name odd-sounding, but if she had judged him correctly, he would keep his word and say nothing of their little secret.

'And you say you found it on her table?' the captain said to Ducamp with that characteristic note of incredulity.

But Didier knew Brook's manner of fishing for lies. In a low, even voice, he returned: 'Aye, when I went to get my wound closed.'

Brook nodded his head slowly, which allowed May to nip in and steer the captain away from unwelcome suspicion. She said: 'But were you not to take me back to Port-de-Paix in exchange for a ransom, Captain?'

'Well, Ladyship,' said Brook, nodding his head slowly, 'there's been a change of plan. See, I don't speak much Spanish, but I can decipher enough of it to know there's enough Spanish silver in Saint Augustine to merit a change of course.'

'We'll be needing to refit the ship,' put in Ducamp.

'Oh, then you might consider leaving me at Charles Town,' added May as if inspired.

Brook let out a deep, amused chuckle at the lady's audacity. He was about to retort when there came a spluttering of coughs from behind. The captain swung round to his portside aft, where Joe, the mulatto, lay open-eyed in an alcove bunk, having lost the glazed look of a dying man. 'Joe, me lad!' cried Brook in a sudden display of gentle cheerfulness, a sound that Ducamp had never heard from the throat of Ned Brook before, and one that seemed to May to be at odds with his character. Then he reached for a bottle on the table and poured out a glass of rum.

Meanwhile, May strode over to the mulatto's bunk side. She touched his forehead, and in a maternal tone, she said: 'His fever has abated.'

'Here, give 'im some o' this, it'll knock 'im right again.'

'Captain, it certainly will not. It's probably what aggravated his illness in the first place!'

'Nothing wrong with rum, natural sugars turned into alcohol, and alcohol preserves, Ladyship . . .'

'It also weakens one's natural defences. He needs to be strong, not drunk!'

'And how would a fine lady know that?'

'My father was a physician,' lied May. In truth, she had picked up the art of concocting poisons and draughts from an old half-Taino, half-Spanish maid in Havana. In this New World a girl had to know how to look after herself.

'Suit yourself,' said the captain, and downed the drink himself.

'I need you to prop him up so his blood flows up and down; otherwise, it will lie stagnant, and he will need bloodletting,' said May, making it all sound very learned. Brook slammed down his empty glass on the table and strode back to the bunk to prop the mulatto up. Gently, he placed his large hands on either side of Joe's slender torso, and, being careful not to bump Joe's head on the timber frame, he lifted him into the sitting position.

'Thank you, Captain,' said Joe, feebly placing a slender hand on Brook's thick wrist.

'By thunder, Joe, me boy,' blurted Brook, 'thought you was a goner!' Brook took Joe's hand and with modesty laid it by the mulatto's side. 'Don't worry, Joe. We've got you covered,' pursued Brook, visibly cheered to see his mulatto sitting up.

May suddenly realised that Joe meant much more to the captain than she initially thought, that she could make him her ticket to a safe haven. After a fleeting glance at Ducamp, she said to Brook: 'I think he is over the worst. He needs food, and I will need to make him up a proper draught to enhance the humours. Otherwise, there's a chance he might relapse.'

'If I didn't know any better, I'd say you were sent by the devil himself,' said Brook in his gravelly voice, now jovial, 'with your draughts and your missive of silver . . . You're my flaming red diablo!' Then, turning to Didier, he said: 'What d'you say, bosun?'

'I'd say she wants to get the hell out of here.'

'All right, then, Ladyship. I'll tell you what: you put my Joe right, and we have a deal. We'll take you to Charles Town. Besides, we'll probably fetch a better price with your own family than with your uncle *par alliance,* hah!'

May had not thought of that possibility. It had not occurred to her that he might try to ransom her elsewhere. She wished she had not mentioned Charles Town, and she almost blurted out that her father was dead. But then she held herself back, realising that it would be one lie too many. For well May new, telling lies, like making draughts, was all about dosage. Overdo it, and you ran the risk of ruining all the benefit. Nevertheless, she was not dissatisfied with her afternoon's work. Not only had she gained an ally in Ducamp, she had found a way of gaining, if not the captain's respect, at least his acceptance. She had both retained her ladyship status and acquired that of diablo. She had better not let him down, she thought to herself; she would just have to play it by ear.

Just as she was rejoicing inside at the thought of regaining the port of Charles Town, the captain looked up again from Joe and said: 'But first, we head for Saint Augustine!'

'What about refurbishing the ship?' said Ducamp, sensing the lady's disappointment.

'No time, bosun, but we'll put it to the vote!'

*

An hour later found May about to give Joe the draught composed of wine, lemon juice, and laudanum that she had concocted.

But she paused, put the mixture on the table, and went to the window to listen to the voice of Captain Brook that boomed from the quarterdeck. He was addressing the crew. She had been anxiously waiting for him to put to the vote whether to make their next port of call Charles Town or not.

'To yer liking, is she, lads?' he bayed. The question was instantly answered with a collective 'Aye, Captain!' Brook scanned the host of cheering men with his beady eyes. 'Johnny Reed,' he hurled, reaching out a crooked forefinger over the balustrade, 'what's your verdict?'

'A fine rover, Cap'n, well balanced and sits well!' called back the helmsman.

'We'll be needing to cut more ports for the cannons, though,' called out gunner Robbins.

'Aye, that we'll do, once we put in at Charles Town,' replied Brook.

'And we'll need to remove the deck houses to make a clean sweep of the deck,' said Billy Hawkes, perched in the rigging.

'Right you are, Billy boy!' returned Brook, capping his forehead with his hand. 'We'll make her fit for a career!' Then, turning back to the group on deck below, he said: 'Pedro, your verdict, man!'

'I agree, a fine rover,' returned Pedro Morales in a strong accent. 'But she be of a deeper draught, Capitán.'

'Aye,' said Brook. 'We won't wanna be hugging the coast as close as before!'

'Long as that's clear, then she'll be a fine sailor, me thinks,' added Pedro.

'And best of all,' called out the fat cook, his back against the main mast to take the weight off his peg leg, 'her storeroom's chock-full for a month of roving!'

There came another cheer of approval.

'So far, so good,' thought May, standing nervously behind the window. They had unanimously indicated that the ship needed to be refitted, and the obvious port of call would be Charles Town.

Outside, before the quarterdeck balustrade, Brook held up a hand. 'Right, lads,' he pursued once the uproar had abated, 'how's about we try out her marauding powers?'

'She'll need fitting out first, Cap'n,' said a bald-headed sailor.

'Of course she will,' said May from inside the cabin.

'Aye, I agree, Jack Hargrave, but I've come across some intelligence that might make yers wanna act on the spur. That is, if you're still game to line your filthy pockets with silver! Are yer with me?'

May's heart sank in her bosom as another roar of assent rose up from the main deck and the rigging like a roaring wind.

'We're a' listening, Cap'n,' said Jack Hargrave.

'There be silver bars salvaged from a sunken Spanish payroll ship. And guess what, lads? I happen to know where they been stored, and it ain't in Havana! No, they've stowed 'em away in Saint Augustine. Now, all you swabbers who ain't seen much of these parts o' the world need to know that Saint Augustine is a tiny settlement compared to Havana. If we were to slip in now, and we ain't far, we could sack the town and take away the silver before the Spaniards even left Havana, now that they're busy with a war on their hands!'

'But there be gun batteries at that port, I know for a fact,' said a seasoned salt by the name of Jimmy Robbins.

'*Si, si*, Jim is right. They are building a presidio,' seconded Pedro Morales, himself a Spaniard.

'Then we'll enter under Spanish colours, won't we?' blasted Brook, his thunderous glare defying any challenge. 'Easy pickings for the brave, lads, easier than the one we did on Cuba because we run straight into port; there's no hiking 'cross country. Besides, I wager me good looks that's what the Frenchies were planning before we blew 'em to kingdom come! Now, are yers up to the challenge?'

A great cheer of assent carried through the cedar timbers into the cabin where May had been taking care of Joe. She now sat in a daze, looking into mid-distance as it dawned on her that the ship she had seen leave port at Port-de-Paix was lost and all hands with it. All those young men barely out of boyhood, whose mothers were probably still praying for their safe return, dead.

She felt sick, as if someone had punched her in the stomach while pregnant. How awful to lose a child, she thought. To lose it in childbirth was one thing, but to lose one you had raised, fed, and loved must be unbearable.

She never thought she would be much of a mother when she had found out she was pregnant. She remembered not being at all reluctant to let her nanny do much of the care work, and then let Mrs Moore take care of Lily-Anne so she could earn a living overseas. She nonetheless loved her daughter profoundly, and thinking of her made her feel both anxious and guilty. Could all her secret prayers for her daughter's wellbeing be in vain too?

'Somethin' up, Ladyship?' said Joe in his calming, sweet voice. 'You wanna go home, but you can't?'

'Yes, Joe, yes, that's it,' said May, taking up the draught again from the table. 'I was hoping to get to Charles Town first.'

'I know how you feel; I wanna go home sometimes too. I got brothers, I got sisters . . .'

'Is that why you fell ill, Joe?' said May. 'You felt homesick?'

'It is, Ladyship, but I'm glad you here now. We can miss home together, yes?'

May never thought one day she would be a sitter for a young mulatto, let alone become an accomplice to a raid on a Spanish port. She hoped she would not die on this ship, that she would not get blown up, or worse, captured and tried for piracy. But most of all, she hoped she would see her child again. 'Yes, Joe, we can miss home together,' said May, and gave him the draught.

SEVEN

OVER THE ENSUING days, Didier began to feel uncommonly on edge.

Every time he saw the lady exchanging a word with a band of mates, he felt a sudden pang of anxiety, and stood poised to jump to her aid at the first sign of a misplaced gesture. If only the woman would keep to her cabin, he would say to himself as they tacked against the westerlies. They were nonetheless making a good five knots and logging one hundred miles from dawn to dusk.

Could he be falling for one such as she? he wondered one day as a large, beautiful butterfly landed on the deck rail. Its visit generally meant they would soon be sighting land. He told himself again there was nothing more enticing, disenchanting, and enslaving than love for a woman. Besides, he had a fortune to be made before he embarked on finding one. Moreover, an impossible love it would be, for even in this New World, a commoner could not engage feelings with a noblewoman, any more than a moth could court a butterfly.

'So, Lieutenant, how long do you think you can go on killing for a livelihood?' said May without irony later that same morning, on the subject of their imminent arrival at Saint Augustine. She and Ducamp were standing on the main deck. She had come out for air as she often did, her cabin being like a sweatbox despite her trying to screen the windows from the intense rays of the sun. Moreover, it would soon be time for her to saunter along to the steaming kitchen at the forecastle to fetch Joe's grub and the wine she needed to make up his draught.

Ducamp noticed she now dressed in garments that were looser fitting, though her shapely figure was still a constant strain, what with a shipload of sex-starved sailors to contend with. However, he continued to keep his reserve about her wanderings to himself.

But it was no secret to the crew that the French soldier had an interest, if not a flame, which, his being the bosun, and a big one at that, gave her breathing space. That was not to say she did not have to turn her eyes from men with a hand down their breaches on a number of occasions.

As for the captain, except for a tart from time to time, he had no time for women. He would much rather have a hull full of treasure than a harem of painted ladies whose charms were quickly spent. And he much preferred the musty smell of silver to sweet perfume.

'We don't kill for our livelihood,' returned Ducamp to May. 'We avoid it whenever we can.'

'You mean when anyone tries to defend their home and the hard-earned fruits of their labours!'

'We rob from those who steal from these lands. And there's no bigger thief than the Spanish Crown!'

'But there are women and children in Saint Augustine as there are settlers in every port, Lieutenant.'

'They won't be harmed if they cooperate, Madame,' said

Ducamp, more sternly than he meant to sound. She had tickled a nerve. For well Ducamp knew from experience what could become of pretty women and innocent folk who showed any resistance. Though he had made a pile of coin on a Cuban foray into the township of Bayamo, he had never forgotten that scene when Captain Brook indulged in his love of torture and slaughter. Didier had watched as Brook made a show of mutilating leading citizens before killing them, under the pretext of putting the fear of the devil into the townspeople to loosen their tongues. Brook had blown off the mayor's face after chopping off an arm, and he had planted an axe in the heart of a man who turned out to be the only doctor for miles around. It had worked, however, and no more killings were carried out. But it had given Ducamp a conscience, and now that the lady brought up the imminent raid, he worried he was losing his feeling of indifference that had so far protected him from remorse and regret. Loss of indifference could put his life in danger for it could affect focus during battle. A solider must learn to kill and forget. It was the golden rule that had guided his career and made him such a redoubtable soldier in France.

May, who knew nothing of the Bayamo episode, was only trying to bond with this man and plumb his depths. Sensing she was delving too deep too quickly, she backed off under the pretext of having to fix Joe's grog.

She had, over the days, gained Captain Brook's respect now that Joe, though sleepy, was on the mend. She suspected, however, that the course of nature and proper alimentation was what had revived her patient as much as her draughts. Nevertheless, she definitely sensed that the captain had lowered his guard around her, a crucial step in her strategy to escape the ship should the occasion arise. And

May had not survived this long in the Caribbean without knowing that when opportunity came knocking, you had to reach out and grab it, and you needed to be in a condition to do so. She would have to make every sailor believe she was incapable of escape, to dull any suspicion. So to prepare dispositions in case the chance of escape did arise, over the past days she had made a point of not being shy to fetch Joe's grub and grog herself from the cook, Hammond, who fell over himself to serve her. This way, the men would become used to her wandering, which she made a point of undertaking generally under the eye of the French lieutenant, without, of course, letting him know. She was clever that way.

As for the captain, he let her roam free, content as he was that Joe was on the mend, and satisfied to have captured a ship that left a straight wake in the sea, as good as a furrow of a well-ploughed field.

As soon as the coast came within view, Brook gave the order to hoist the colours of a Spanish supply ship. Had they been sailing in the sloop, their tactic might well have been suspicious because of the large number of gun ports. But the *Bella Fortuna* had not yet undergone any refitting and appeared as she had been made, as a merchant ship, albeit a merchant ship with sixty treasure-seeking rovers aboard.

They arrived off shore as the night fell, the land breeze forbidding an entry into port. 'Good timing,' thought Captain Brook to himself, for as no one aboard had intelligence about the latest additions to the fort, he was quite content to use the pretext of the late hour to anchor in the roadstead north of the inlet. The harbour chief would not send out a pilot to guide them under darkness; it would be normal practice to wait until daylight. 'So, mates,' hurled the captain from the quarterdeck, 'I say we take 'em tonight. Are yers up for it?' Brook knew as well as every mate aboard that their roar of assent would be carried seaward by the land breeze, well out of earshot of any folk on land.

*

All was calm in the fort settlement. The watchman was sitting by the enclosure fire, puffing cosily at his clay pipe. He gazed up at the night heavens, where the slow-moving clouds recurrently covered the white light of the big moon.

The settlement consisted of a palisade-bound fortress—which enclosed a wooden chapel, garrison buildings, and storehouses—and a cluster of daub and wattle houses that sat outside the palisade wall and led down to the San Juan River. The smallest of these houses, which had just one room, belonged to Pepe Castro.

Pepe Castro was not among those of the fort settlement who groused about the lack of womenfolk, the distance from Havana, and the rudimentary life on the east coast of Florida. On the contrary, he enjoyed the warm climate, the hunting and, most of all, coming as he did from the Galician coastal village of Cangas de Morrazo, he loved the fishing. And here, the fish were like nothing he had ever caught in Spain; here, they were gargantuan in comparison.

Tonight, Pepe would not snore soundly in his little house. He had decided to take advantage of the big moon and the extra-high tide. He was spending a delicious moment in his pirogue, where there already lay three fat bass and a gigantic red fish that he would sell to the garrison cook in the morning. The governor loved his fish spiced with ginger.

The tide would be retreating within the hour, he reckoned, as he gazed up at the moonlit river. That meant another hour's worth of fishing in his favourite spot, where the creek forked into the wetlands from the main river inlet. He was line fishing where the cold water met the warm water, and where the big fish ate the small ones who came feeding. He had positioned his pirogue opposite the moon so that, from a fish's point of view, his silhouette would blend into the dark backdrop of vegetation on the marshy bank. Having felt the catgut line for any excessive stretching, he was about to apply bait to the hook when a sploshing further down the inlet compelled him to look downstream and stare hard.

He could hardly believe his eyes when he realised he was seeing three long rowboats advancing in the moonlight from the wide bend in the sea inlet. 'They must be from the supply ship,' he thought at first, perhaps to reassure himself. But why would they be silently moving upstream like marauding alligators? Then it dawned on him. 'Dios mio!' he let out, now facing the fact that these marauders must be none other than desperados, villains of the sea. What they would be wanting here, he had no idea. He only knew he had to get back quick to give the alert to the garrison of an imminent attack.

Pepe quickly wound up his line and laid down his rod in the bottom of the pirogue. Then he dug into the water with his paddle, hugging the north shore with the marauders barely a gunshot away further downstream. But at some point, he would have to cut across to the other side to join the settlement on the south bank. He kept paddling hard for thirty yards in the skinny water, trying to keep the splash to a minimum, by which time a cloud passed partially over the moon, dimming its light. He would have no better chance to cross over; than now, he thought to himself, the men in the boat would probably not be looking so far ahead of them. So, taking an oblique angle so as not to lose too much of his lead, Pepe paddled for all he was worth as he aimed directly for the south bank settlement, just three hundred yards ahead.

'God's blood! Looks like a boat ahead, Captain!' said Jack Taylor, pointing in the night toward the dark shadow moving swiftly from the cover of the north bank.

'I see the bugger,' growled Brook. He gave the order to the ten oarsman of the *Bella Fortuna* longboat to give chase to prevent the lone rower from getting to shore. He knew that losing the element of surprise would be a major setback and could even jeopardize the whole venture. The other longboat— taken from the *Joseph* and headed by the bosun—and a slower pinnace upped its pace likewise on Brook's signal. All of a sudden, no longer were the oarsmen's sculls slipping soundlessly into the water, but batting it like a waterwheel in a menacing, percussive thrashing.

Pepe glanced over his shoulder as the sudden commotion just two hundred yards to his aft sent his heart racing faster. He had been spotted, and their reaction was the confirmation of their evil intentions. But Pepe was barely fifty yards from the settlement shore. He felt confident in his swift pirogue, which sat low in the water and produced little drag; felt that he could reach it in time. Once ashore, he only had to run to the palisade gate to give the alert.

The night light grew whiter as the moon partly reappeared from behind another cloud. Then, as he glanced back again, his eyes caught a bright flash. It was instantly followed by the appalling crack of a firing musket, and then a dull thud as the lead shot sank into the gunwale. 'Madre de Dios!' cried out Pepe; he had not thought that they could fire and shoot so well. But it might be a lucky shot, he told himself as he instinctively sank his head into his shoulders while digging faster into the water. His hope was dashed when, ten strokes later, a whole cluster of flashes and a splattering of detonations sent wildfowl flapping from the marshy shore as the volley of shots peppered his gunwale, and one sank into his shoulder. 'Aie, Madre!' he hurled out. *I can't die on the day of my record catch*, Pepe thought to himself.

But he could hardly take cover: his only chance was to keep paddling, and pray to the Virgin Mary to help him over the thirty-yard stretch of brackish water that separated him from the settlement shore.

'Marauders, marauders! We're under attack!' he screamed out in the faint hope that someone would hear. Another volley of shots dashed his pirogue; one sank into his upper arm, causing him to nearly lose balance. Despite the pain, Pepe carried on, desperately chopping away the water. The assailants were barely a hundred yards behind and approaching fast. At last, he beached on the slow-sloping foreshore and jumped out of the pirogue. As he did so, he glanced at his fish. The red fish was the biggest he had ever caught in his life. He reached into the pirogue and hooked his fingers under its gills. As he pulled it away, he came under fire and took a shot in the thigh. He ducked away, still carrying his fish, and hobbled as fast as he could past the first daub and wattle houses along the short earth track that led up to the palisade. He yelled at the top of his voice between heartburning gasps. '*Ladrones, ladrones!* We're under attack! Wake up! We're under attack!'

Coming level with his little house that stood thirty yards before the palisade, he turned and saw the villains jumping ashore. He wondered for a moment if he should fetch his musket or keep hobbling to the palisade gate.

On making footfall on the settlement shore, Brook quickly scanned the moonlit track and the modest dwellings before it. He squeezed his genitals that were stinging from sitting in the boat, and he was maddened. He saw the lone rower had stopped and was standing at the far end, an irresistible target for any man in battle mode. 'Davy, shoot the bastard!' said Brook irately, turning to a sailor with a musket. The rover went down on one knee while the target went hobbling off again toward the palisade gate.

Brook thought to himself that something was not quite right. He imagined the settlement to be less rustic than it looked now under the white light of the moon. Even the palisade looked like nothing more than a line of stakes hammered into the ground. This would be like taking biscuit from a babe, he thought to himself. His contemplation was interrupted by a loud detonation, and Brook turned his sharp eye on the target as the lead shot went whistling through the air. He loved that instant of suspense between the bullet leaving the barrel and reaching its target, or not.

A second later, Pepe Castro from Cangas de Morrazo, who loved fishing, felt a powerful thud in the back that kicked the breath out of him. He fell, face down, with the biggest red fish he had ever caught in his life, a life cut short by a stranger's bullet.

Brook wondered how many soldiers there were inside the fort. There was only one way to find out, and he knew that speed was of the essence now that the bell was ringing out from the enclosure. But that was all right, he thought to himself; he had a plan. He slapped Davy in a comradely fashion on the cheek. 'Nearly thought you'd lost it, man!'

Then he turned to see the bosun who was jumping ashore from the second longboat.

Before the captain could speak, Ducamp said sternly: 'He'd already raised the alarm. There was no need to kill him!'

Brook growled back: 'Cap'n's orders, bosun!' Didier knew what that meant. Once the assault had started, the captain's word was final; it was written in the ship's articles. 'Look, man, it'll stop anyone else from trying to get in through the gate,' said Brook, laying a heavy hand on Ducamp's shoulder. Then, in a more confidential tone, he added: 'Palisade up ahead, houses left and right; they've got a clear shot, but if we're quick, we got hostages. And you can bet they're shittin' bricks inside their little shacks and now too scared to run for the palisade. Get it?'

'No civilians, we agreed,' said Ducamp, unmoved by Brook's reasoning.

'Look, we draw out the commander, and if he has any moral fibre, he surrenders, and we take the silver without any casualties. Trust in your ole sea-salty Cap'n, bosun. Done it before, and it works, man . . .' Brook slapped Ducamp's shoulder while turning to the rest of the men leaping out of boats and gathering along the shore. 'Remember, lads,' he said with one eye on the bosun, 'we come for the silver and nought else, and then get the hell out of here!'

'Aye, Cap'n!'

Turning back to Ducamp, he said: 'There. Now, you take the houses on the right, run round the back. Shake 'em from their cots and bring 'em all out!' Ducamp gave a curt nod. Then, turning to the group, Brook said: 'Frank, Mossa, Jake, Davy, you keep a musket on the palisade. They show their heads, tickle their ears!'

The quartermaster being dead, Didier took command of his boatload of mates along with half the mates of the pinnace. These included some of the new French recruits. In all he led two dozen men around the back of the houses, which offered intermittent screens from potential fire from the palisade, especially as the moon now glimmered brightly. It was as good as daylight to the accustomed eye, and formed deep shadows near vegetation and buildings, which was as much an advantage as a disadvantage. It gave clear vision, but it also meant they could be picked out in the open. On reaching each house, Ducamp motioned to three men to peel off the pack and take it. He then led the remaining party to the next house up, leaving behind the sounds of women screaming, men protesting, and young children confused and braying. Casting a glance back over his shoulder at the first of the captives being marched, pushed, or dragged from their homes, he determined that these people must be mostly indentured workers and farmers.

All the while, the garrison soldiers inside the fort were jumping in their boots and grabbing their arms under the hurled orders of their superior. But the pirate crack shooters kept soldiers heads down behind the palisade as Ducamp now reached the last of the houses nearest the palisade gate. With him were Billy Hawkes and Jack Hargraves.

He motioned to Billy and Jack to stand on either side of the door; then he kicked it in. 'Fuera y no les hacemos daño!' he ordered in his deep, stern voice. It was one of the Spanish phrases he had picked up on his first raid in Cuba. He did not know what each word meant, just that it told the occupants to get out and they would not be harmed, and that it usually worked better when he was not brandishing his cutlass. So he stood filling the doorway, his eyes searching in the darkness.

He instantly detected the smell of a newborn baby as his gaze fell upon a flurry of movement under the roughhewn table. In the night light that streamed from the open door, he spied a woman holding a bundle close to her bosom as if she were trying to keep it from braying. He bent down slightly and reached out a hand. Suddenly, his peripheral vision detected rapid movement from inside the doorframe to his right. With a battle-trained reflex, he pulled back his head from a striking knife. Sidestepping left, he followed up with his right hand that clasped the back of the assailant's thick wrist. Then he twisted it into the man's body while pulling hard on his arm. The stocky Spaniard, his eyes desperate and fearful, let out a cry. Ducamp's manoeuvre had caused the man's shoulder to dislocate, and he dropped his knife. Though strong, this man was no fighter. Instead of killing him, Ducamp quickly spun round and held his neck in the crook of his arm. 'Calmete, hombre!' he hurled, squeezing the man until he stopped writhing. 'We won't hurt you. Just come calmly! *Entiendes?*'

The Spaniard gave a tense-faced jerk of the head to communicate his assent, his face twisted with the pain of the dislocation.

'Good man!' said Ducamp, then slowly released the Spaniard's neck from the powerful hold. The man was defeated; there was no need to inflict further humiliation. He had done what any man should do: he had tried to protect his family from the invader. Ducamp gestured to the woman to come out from the under the table and exit the house.

'No te preocupes!' he said, another expression he had picked up which told the young woman not to worry.

She returned a frightened scowl. How could she trust a man

who had invaded her home? Nonetheless, she cautiously got out from under the table while placing her lips on the down on the baby's head. The child coughed, gasped for air a long moment, and then let out a powerful cry.

As he marched them toward the shore where the hostages were being assembled, Ducamp heard deep-voiced protests and the muffled scream of a woman from inside a house. He told Billy Hawkes to take over, then kicked open the door that had been left ajar.

The shutter had been thrown open on the other side of the room to let in the light of the moon. He immediately saw two mates restraining a bald peasant. A knife was pressed to his throat, his head held so he faced the bed. Ducamp recognised the big, bullish head and stocky build of one of the new recruits, the one called Mattis. He was on top of a woman whose shift had been ripped at the throat, his face buried between her generous breasts. His right hand was visibly guiding his cock between her thighs as she lay tense but visibly powerless in the knowledge that her husband's life depended on her submission.

'Relâchez-le!' hurled Ducamp, who recognised the two mates as new recruits from the *Bella Fortuna*. He continued his stride to the bed and pulled Mattis away by the scruff of his collar. As with his mercenary soldiers back home in France, he knew that if he wanted to keep men from rebelling, he would have to refrain from being judgemental. So he let Mattis recover his feet, pull up his breeches, and put away his erect cock. 'For Christ's sake, man!' said Ducamp.

'I found her first!' snarled Mattis, who had evidently gotten the wrong impression.

'She's no one's, man!' said Ducamp. 'Have you forgotten? We're here for just one thing, the bloody silver!'

Five minutes later, the rabble of subdued and scared hostages was being marched up the dirt track to the palisade. A dozen rovers had their muskets cocked and aimed at the palisade wall, while Captain Brook marched directly behind the human shield. 'Line 'em up in front,' said Brook as they approached the fort gate, where Pepe the fisherman lay as dead as his big red fish.

Amid the shrieks of frightened women, many still in their shifts, an accented and mature voice yelled out from behind the palisade gate. 'Who are you, and what do you want?'

'Never mind who we are,' thundered Brook. 'You know what we want and we want it now! Just hand over the silver, and we'll leave you and these good people in peace. If not, they will die, and you'll be next!'

Crude but ever effective, thought Ducamp, standing a few yards from Brook, and towering over the little people before him. It occurred to him that he would not allow these people to be killed. But of course Brook was bluffing, wasn't he?

'We know you're outnumbered, or you'd have attacked us, unless your love for silver is stronger than the love of your fellow countrymen? What say you, Governor?'

Brook's demand was met with silence from the fortress. After an agonising minute of frightened sniffles on the backdrop of chirping insects of the night, the captain called out again. 'We're still 'ere, Governor, and we ain't going away. What say you?' Again a minute of silence followed. Brook then motioned to Billy Hawkes to bring his hostage forward. Ducamp saw it was the bald Spaniard who had been forced to watch the attempted rape of his wife. A woman screamed out, 'Es mi marido, por dios, no le matan, por favor, tenemos niños!' She grabbed her husband desperately by the sleeve. Ducamp knew that "niños" meant children. It occurred to him that her children must still be hiding in the house. But he let it drop as Mattis pulled her back and promptly dumped her five yards back. 'Shut it, or you'll be next!' he told her as she began to wail on her knees with her head in her hands.

Captain Brook had told the bosun that the civilians would not be involved, so surely this was part of the bluff. Ducamp had figured too that the garrison must only comprise a small contingent of soldiers; otherwise, the governor would surely have attacked while they were rounding up the settlers, he thought. There again, it would make sense that the governor had not reacted against the assault, as he would be held to account if he lost the precious payroll treasure, in which case, he might indeed value the salvaged silver more than the lives of a handful of indentured colonists. Ducamp suddenly realised that the designated Spaniard was in danger of being shot. But if he intercepted now, it would weaken Brook's position and ruin his bluff. Holding his tongue, Ducamp remained tense, and ready to step in should the need arise.

'What say you, Governor?' repeated Brook, his voice now fraught with restrained rage. Then, after half a dozen heartbeats, he boomed: 'Speak up, or this man's death will be on your conscience!'

At last, the governor called out in a passionate claim. 'I swear to God, we have no silver here!'

But the captain was nobody's fool. It seemed to him that they would need to set an example of their determination. 'All right,' he called back. Then he turned to the bald Spaniard who was feverishly crossing himself between Mattis and Billy Hawkes. 'Adelante, walk toward the gate!' he growled. The Spaniard, amid pokes and jeers from his captors, began walking feebly to the timber gate.

It soon became clear to Mattis why the Spaniard took such small steps. 'Bwah, he's shit himself!' he blurted out with an amused jeer. Brook noticed with relish that the new French recruit was enjoying his newfound freedom to do whatever misdemeanours he could revel in, and Brook liked to have kindred spirits aboard his ship. 'Hah, don't worry, *hombre*,' added Mattis. 'We'll take care of your lady!'

The captain snarled sardonically and pulled a pistol on the Spaniard to encourage him to keep walking. 'I'm waiting, Governor, and I'm not a patient man! In twelve paces, this man dies. So what say you?'

'We have no silver here!' called back the governor with more urgency.

Brook, sensing his usual tactics would pay dividends, began counting the Spaniard's steps as he walked toward the fisherman, lying dead on the ground with his fish. 'Twelve. Eleven. Ten . . .' He was enjoying the moment, entertaining the lads, most of whom joined in the countdown. Ducamp was not among them; the governor would give in first, he thought to himself. After all, he had no choice: he was undermanned, the fortress primitive; it would not take more than a few grenades and an axe to hack through that gate. There again, maybe he was being over optimistic, so he stepped forward, ready to call a halt to the madness even though it would go against the custom of the coast.

The count continued, and the captain had that terrible glint in his eye of a man on the brink of fulfilling a deep desire. 'Nine. Eight. Seven . . .' He flitted his eyes sideways and caught sight of the approaching bosun. 'Your call, Governor!' Brook called out and cocked his flintlock. The count continued. 'Six. Five . . .' Still no answer as the raiders' captives looked on with bated breath. Brook took aim. On 'three,' he fired, and the Spanish settler dropped like a stone. 'Ha, ha, surprise!' boomed out Brook triumphantly to his men in a bout of macabre chortling. But a dreadful, visceral scream from the man's wife covered the captain's laugh, as the other hostages gasped and whimpered with dread, their hands covering their mouths in shock and horror. The ruthless captain had jumped the gun and had tricked the whole gallery, including his own men.

Mattis gave an amazed chuckle as he pointed to the Spaniard who lay next to the corpse of Pepe and his big red fish. The new recruit was manifestly looking forward to a bout as a rover, now that he had confirmation that anything was permitted. He could revel in sin and get away with it. He had found his natural family, he thought to himself, and it was exciting. Brook then motioned with the muzzle of his pistol to Mattis to bring another villager forward from the herd. Mattis glanced defiantly up at Ducamp and grabbed the man who the bosun had taken prisoner.

'Not this one!' said Didier.

But Brook growled back: 'Let him come!' With a smirk of derision, Mattis grabbed the Spaniard who yelled out with the pain from his dislocated shoulder and pushed him into the solitary space between the group and the palisade gate. 'Keep walking, *hombre!*' said Brook to the Spaniard, who had halted. The man looked back at his wife and child and crossed himself before Mattis pushed him into step. The woman glanced at Ducamp with a look of fear and disdain as the captain slipped his musket into his leather holster and pulled out another. 'Once we're finished, we're coming for you, Governor. Last chance or no quarter!' he growled playfully. Then he pulled back the cock and took aim as the countdown began. 'Twelve . . . eleven, ten . . .'

That malicious twinkle in the captain's eye, the lustful scowl that curled his upper lip, told Ducamp that Brook would try to surprise everyone again. As Didier was about to take another step forward to come within grabbing distance of the gun barrel, the governor's voice broke out from behind the palisade.

'Wait! We will surrender, but we have no silver. No silver here, I say!'

'Wrong answer!' boomed Brook. 'We know about the salvage operation!'

'No, that is in San Augustin,' returned the governor at once, his voice losing its sternness. 'We have none of it here.'

'San Augustin,' said Brook deadpan, pulling back his outstretched arm. 'Where the bloody hell's this, then?'

'This is *el forte* San Mateo, not San Augustin! San Augustin is further south.'

Brook turned to his men. 'Bloody hell's bells!' he boomed out. Then, turning back to the palisade gate, he called: 'Come out, lay down your arms, and we'll leave you in peace.'

*

The first flies invaded the dead fish and laid eggs in the eye sockets of Pepe the fisherman.

Meanwhile, one foresighted soldier was trying to pick the lock of the prison cell door where he had been crammed with over a score of his comrades.

The three dozen settlers were shut up in the little chapel, and the wailing wife of the bald man had collapsed into a grieving slumber at the altar. Three thick timbers had been

96

nailed to the doorframe on the outside to delay the occupants' escape.

It had all been a foolish mistake, a futile effort, thought Ducamp, though none of the rovers brought it up as they rowed back to the *Bella Fortuna*.

Mattis, for one, was not displeased with his first foray as a dastardly sea dog. He had at least gotten a taste of the sinful pleasures to come despite the bosun's meddling, and he had gained the captain's favour.

Ducamp, however, got to thinking about the colonist sacrificed to get the governor to surrender. Did Ned Brook have any human feeling at all? he wondered. Killing a man in battle was a God-given right, and he had done his fair share of killing. But killing a man in cold blood as a sacrificial rite and procuring pleasure from it was more than the bosun could comprehend. Perched at the stern of the longboat as the night began to pale, Didier wondered when he had turned, become numb to humanity, become a ruthless pirate.

He had signed up as privateer subsequent to deserting the French army. He had been obliged to apply pressure on his own countrymen on the whim of the king. Occupying Huguenot bourgeois homes had been an eye-opening experience. But the novelty of peering into their habitat had quickly worn off; and it had become tedious, if not sickening, to harass these countrymen whose only crime was to believe in God, without artifice, the way they personally saw fit. Their belief was chosen, not imposed, given that their Bibles were in the language of the people instead of in Latin. But as he thought about it, was his situation any better now, waging war as he was solely for personal gain, impervious to injustice and under the orders of a tyrant?

How could he have let it happen? he wondered, as the men silently sculled in the wake of the captain's longboat. What wind had blown him off course? In these lands, like many a man on foreign soil, he had lost his moral compass, and in the fresh early morning, it now felt unclean to raid, loot, and kill in this way. They had made off with a token sack of jewellery, some gunpowder, and a sack full of lentils for the ruin of their souls.

'Too good to be true, eh?' said Billy Hawkes glumly to his neighbour.

'Aye, but one thing's come of it, though,' returned Jack Hargraves. 'We now got confirmation the silver's in Saint Augustine, i'n't we!'

EIGHT

'BAH, IT HAPPENS, man, stupid mistake,' said Captain Brook, slapping a comradely hand on the bosun's back as he climbed aboard. 'Coz we are *stupidos*, ha-ha!'

The captain turned with a sardonic eye to the mates who had boarded from the longboat before Ducamp. They were won over by the self-derision and chortled in return.

But Ducamp's closed expression was not due to the lack of decent loot. His mind was on the sacrifice. It was cruel and, so it turned out, needless.

Brook did not like long faces of discontent, and he could smell discontent in a man's sweat. It could lead to dissention if it was not nipped in the bud. Besides, everyone ought to be rejoicing, for they now had the certitude that the silver was attainable, which should fire up their fighting spirits. 'In every cloud, ain't there a silver lining, bosun? So just keep with it, and this one will be raining silver coins!' said the captain in a growl while peering right into the bosun's face. 'Unless you're getting cold feet.' It was his favourite trick to draw out the truth of a man's ponderings.

Ducamp looked back levelly into the captain's dark eyes. He was in no mood for false pretense; he had to get it off his chest, so he said: 'There was no need to execute the Spaniard. You'd a left more time, and the governor would'a surrendered. There weren't even two dozen of them.'

'We didn't know that, did we, clever cogs, unless you can see into the future!' said Brook. He did not appreciate having to justify himself, but he knew it was important to make the effort when there was the smell of rebellion in the air. 'I was aiming for his bloody shoulder if it'll make yer feel any better, bosun. Besides, it was a clean shot. Felt it the moment it left the barrel, and he didn't feel a thing, and now he's gone. End of story!'

But Didier was not done yet. He said: 'I might be a soldier by trade, but I ain't never killed for the sake of getting a sweet shot!'

'It's the sacrifice. I told yer, kill one or two from the outset, and you avoid conflict, and save the lives, ours and theirs. Ain't that right, lads?'

There came a charge of 'ayes,' but Ducamp was not listening to background noises; neither did he hear the rush of the calm sea and the squawk of gulls. He said: 'It's killing innocent people . . . The man had a wife and kids!'

The scowl upon Brook's face grew thinner. His eyes glowed black. The bosun had made his point; why was he looking for a fight? He grabbed Didier firmly by the lapel. 'What's wrong, gone soft in the belly, man, 'ave yer? 'Cause if you have, there ain't no place aboard this ship for a bosun with the runs!'

Ducamp knew he ought to let the man's flare of anger die, but it did not tally with his nature to stand down. Instead, he growled back. 'I signed as a privateer, not as a bloodthirsty pirate!' In a swift up and outward movement of the arms, he freed himself from the captain's grip.

Brook, his face cast in anger, took a step back and pulled out a flintlock from his baldric holster. 'You'll strike yer Cap'n, will yer?' he thundered. Turning to Mattis and a few others standing nearby, he cried out: 'Hold 'im, lads! Take his weapons, and tie him to the main mast! I'll teach him to swipe his captain . . .'

That was unjust, thought Ducamp; he had simply swiped Brook's hands from his lapels. He knew there was no point in arguing, however, so he positioned himself to fight off any assailant. But Mattis, who no doubt saw his chance of a promotion, directed five matelots to surround the offender, with two more standing by to bind his hands. It took them all to hold the bosun down, and in the end, Ducamp realised there was no point rowing against the current. Mattis tied his hands, a wry smile on his lips in the assumption that a bosun's position was about to become vacant, and he knew the ship better than any aboard, having served as bosun under the late Captain Reners.

The grey light of early morning now dispelled any dregs of the night as the ship's mast swayed gently with the incoming tide in the roadstead. It was a good sea for a thrashing, for the aim would not be troubled.

Brook was keen to sail out, but he knew, too, he had to act swiftly to put out any hotbeds of rebellion that likeminded mates might harbour in their hearts. 'Yer a good man, bosun,' he said from the quarterdeck, 'but you know the rules of this ship.' He raised his voice as he swept his gaze around the mates gathered before the mast. 'So let's get it done with and be gone to fetch our silver!'

A few moments later, Brook strode back from his cabin, holding the cat-o'-nine-tails. May followed behind him. 'You know the price for striking yer captain, bosun,' he said, running the leather strands through his left hand to the knotted ends as he sauntered toward the quarterdeck bulustrade. 'Just count your lucky stars you didn't go the way of the Spaniard! Although a bullet in the brain don't hurt; this'll hurt like hell. But let's hope it'll thrash some sense into yers!' Brook tossed the whip to Billy Hawkes.

'Wait,' said Ducamp, 'first off, I didn't swipe my captain. Second, I demand a parley.'

'Parleyin's with the enemy. But I'll call for a parley, provided one o' the boys thinks he's got time to step forward to parley on your behalf.' Brook glared around at the crew members assembled around the main mast. Not a living soul stepped forward in the bosun's defence. For well Brook knew that silver was what was on their minds now, and the faster they got the whipping out of the way, the faster they could get their hands on it. Strutting before the men, Brook roared out in triumph: 'Who's yer Cap'n, lads?'

'You are, Captain!' returned the crew, the voice of Mattis rising above them all.

'Who's gonna lead yers to silver?'

'You are, Captain!'

*

While the bosun lay stripped to the waist, belly to the floor of his cell so his shirt would not cling to his lacerated back, the captain had called for an assembly above deck.

Having forced his way through the ranks before snatching ship and crew from his captain, Ned Brook governed his ship with an iron fist and gut feeling. He well knew the importance of testing the will of the men and reaffirming his authority. Ducamp had been popular enough, renowned for his fair-mindedness. The captain did not want the bosun's little rant to find a breeding ground aboard his ship and to worm its way between the ears of the men. But one thing he could count on was that the sound of silver coins would ring louder in their wax-filled ears than any misplaced sense of fair play. Some of these men would sell their own mother for a pocketful of Spanish dollars. There was nothing better for a crew than to show your command of the situation and make them believe that you were the only man who could lead them.

So, weighing a handful of pieces of eight from his personal collection in his left hand, he told them they could be at Saint Augustine by eventide. The land breeze would keep them away from the coast and help them tack southward. But they would be hard-pushed to reach the port town before a Spaniard travelling on horseback from San Mateo. And with hindsight, he realised that it was very possible that the governor had stalled in order to send a messenger the back way before he had surrendered.

'So lads, change of plan!' Brook thundered, taking his usual stance at the balustrade. 'If we try sailing into port, chances are we'll be smashed to kingdom come by the land guns. So what do we do?' Here, being the natural rouser he was, he paused for effect. Then, weighing his coins in his right hand, he said: 'We put in further down the coast at Matanzas Inlet. Then we surprise the bastards by land from the south! That's what we do!'

'I heard it's a dangerous place, Captain. It's where ole Grammont and Brigaut copped it, cause o' the sandbars there.'

'And that may be, Jack Hargraves, but good news is, I know 'em for sure!'

Now that the men were well fed and in better fettle,

enthusiasm for the plan was not lacking. Collecting the fortune of a payroll ship before the Spanish reinforcements got wind was closer to their hearts than ever, for a payroll ship would have carried tons of silver coin.

Brook's mind was at ease now that he had things under control, now that Joe was on the mend, and that he and the crew had applied the medicine that eased their sores. It was reassuring to know he had months' worth of ingredients with which to concoct the special lotion; the abominable discomfort would also be under control.

*

May had already got the measure of Brook, whom she suspected of being easily prone to fits of blind fury.

She had seen such rage in men before, made worse when they had some incessant worry drilling into their mind, such as a dangerous debt, a heavy burden, or a recurring ailment. It stopped them from thinking clearly as it overshadowed everything in their lives, and crowded their minds so that frustrations could only be evacuated physically. A clenched fist, a visceral roar, the thrust of a boot, or the downward swish of a blade. Once the frustration was vented, space was freed for more reasoned thought. This she had seen in her own late husband, who had a terrible temper made worse with booze and when his secret ailment was giving him gyp.

She had later learnt to use such fury to her advantage with restless men of breeding, frustrated by their hierarchy, their crew, or their own high expectations of their limited capabilities. May knew how a woman's touch could give a chaotic soul the soothing balm to calm the rage that consumed all rational thought. She knew how to let it run its course until the folly subsided while at the same time—

and this was the trick—remaining feisty and sharp, yet without countering the anger, rather coaxing it out like an exorcism, empathizing with frustrations, and drawing out anxieties. For these men were truly possessed, and a drop of laudanum slipped into a drink always helped. Then, on many an occasion, the possessed would become just a boy in need of a sympathetic ear or reassuring word, a sweet kiss or a lover's caress, before a peaceful slumber befell him. Once he was thus tamed, she could add another protector to her string of high-ranking admirers.

It was from such raging, vengeful, frustrated souls that she had obtained her most lucrative morsels of intelligence. Sitting in front of her medicine chest full of carefully labelled glass vessels, she recalled now that it was from one such a frightful, albeit charming, Spanish officer, Capitán Lozano de Torres, that in Havana she had lifted the letter she had shown to the French governor in exchange for a passage to Charles Town. He had pent up his fury at having to stand by to run with the perfidious English against the French in the Antilles, rather than being allowed to fetch the payroll silver from Saint Augustine.

Thinking about it, how she had navigated these dangerous waters, still amazed her. She sometimes wondered how her mother would see her now, her French seamstress mother who died young, leaving her only daughter with just her linguistic and dressmaking skills as her only baggage. May recalled how she, like her mother, had entered adult life as a seamstress. However, that was where the resemblance in their career paths ended. May well remembered how, in want of extra income to adorn her pretty figure, she had accepted an offer of doing evening work, filing coins for coiners for whom she also did a bit of "uttering." Uttering was nothing more than passing the altered coins back into the system by purchasing items and receiving bone fide change. She remembered how naively she thought it such an easy way to earn a living. But when the gang she was working with ended up doing the dance of the hangman, she took heed and moved into a less risky sector that would bring in the cash she had become accustomed to. Taking advantage of her natural charm, she learnt how to pick pockets, an art she performed successfully for a number of years, until she was at last caught and sentenced to a short stay in Newgate prison. It was a hellish hole steeped in squalor. She recalled swearing to herself she would rather die than return there.

But on her release, without a penny to her name, she was tempted back into lifting until she was denounced by one of the gang who wanted to save his own skin. After an eloquent and sincere account of her life since becoming orphaned, she was spared the Tyburn jig and instead was sentenced to be transported to the new colony of Virginia. There, she met her beau, who paid up her indenture and whom she married before embarking aboard his ship to the Caribbean, leaving their daughter in safe care outside Charles Town. Jim Stewart was his name. But three months later, he was dangling on the end of a noose, having been unfairly condemned by a British governor for killing a man in self-defence during a drunken brawl. She recalled how it was all expedited very quickly. One minute, they were on their way home with a hold full of provisions and a heads full of plans; the next minute, she was alone and destitute, and missing her child.

And now look at you, she thought to herself as she prepared a draught for the mulatto from the same bottle whose contents had sent men into a deep slumber. Yes, she had survived so far, had learnt to tame the humours of men, and she regretted most of it. But she had remarked how fear of destitution, fear of death, of being murdered, and most of all now, fear of never seeing her child again, could embolden the spirit, could allow one to put aside conventional and moral behaviour and accept a monstrosity in order to make it through. But as her mother used to say, regrets only made you unfriendly, so there wasn't any point in being bogged down by them. She nonetheless hoped she would not have too many of them later. But to be able to live with her past, she knew she would have to start afresh in a new place. Once out of her mad capsule of time, she would learn to live a normal life with normal people in a northern settlement. It was in order to reach that new place as a woman of means that she had learnt how to tame and then manipulate men's blind rage.

But with Brook, there was something else: she sensed him to be of a very different species than the run-of-the-mill short-tempered male. She suspected he was a born killer, a dark champion of violence who found solace in administering pain and death. But not just death. Death without remorse. Ever since she saw him watch Captain Reners being torn apart limb by limb, she had decided that his was the most dangerous and gruesome kind of human nature. Yet, given recent developments, she would have to humour him.

That morning, by the time she had dressed and joined the quarterdeck to see what all the commotion was about, Ducamp was already being held firmly between two thick-armed mates. Mattis, of all people, was tying his hands to the main mast. It was a severe blow to her plans, and she had to make a concentrated effort to conceal her disappointment. For she well knew that if Captain Brook ever suspected she had any sympathy for the bosun's cause, she would not survive the voyage with dignity.

The captain had made it clear that he had no love of women, so she had no hold there. And now that the silver would by far outweigh any ransom, and her only ally was locked up, she found herself in a precarious position indeed. She had felt Captain Brook's eyes upon her, scrutinising her reaction when Ducamp was tied and flogged. Trying though it was to watch a man being beaten, she had forced herself to look impervious to emotion as every man lined up to take his turn with the cat across the bosun's bare back. The first few mates had given only a token couple of lashes. But then it had come to the turn of Mattis.

Taking the cat-o'-nine-tails from the previous mate, he walked up to Ducamp, then slowly ran a finger over the most lashed area where the skin was bruised and raw, but not yet broken. 'I'll show you how to whip a man!' he grunted, knowing that the captain was looking on from the quarterdeck. He measured his run-up, then raised the whip, taking three steps to Ducamp's bare back, and he cracked the tails across the bruised skin. Ducamp seethed in silence. Again Mattis ran his finger over the lashed area while Brook chortled.

Mattis cracked the whip again, this time causing the bosun to cry out in pain as the knotted whip tore into the flesh. Mattis glared up at the quarterdeck with a showman's bow in search of praise, and Brook obliged. 'Ha-ha, you wicked bastard, Mattis!' he chortled. It was the first time, the captain used the new recruit's first name and Mattis was thrilled.

Unable to watch anymore, May lifted her chin as if all this ship nonsense and rabble was below her, and retired to her cabin. Once inside she had to sit down, steady her nerves to keep the tears down as she recalled the bosun's face of contained agony as the knots tore into his flesh.

Her only insurance was to keep Joe in a state of semi-consciousness which would render her presence capital in the eyes of the captain. So she would keep her patient drugged for a mutual benefit. The extra sleep would do Joe good and keep him from harm's reach, and she would retain her raison d'être aboard this ship. But May was not only a sharp thinker. She also had a creative mind, and she had a plan.

A few hours later, the *Bella Fortuna* was tacking down the east coast. Inside the captain's cabin, Joe looked up from his bunk and thanked May as she passed him his draught. His complexion was brighter now, but he seemed quietly content to let himself be mothered by a pretty white lady. His eyes told her he understood her ploy and thanked her for keeping him safe. Brook walked in.

'How is he?'

'Could be better, Captain, but nonetheless on the mend.'

'Good.'

She detected the captain was in a better frame of mind. So she asked if he wanted her to tend to the bosun. She was concerned his stitches had come undone. 'I do not want a man's death on my conscience, Captain.'

Pouring himself his own draught of rumbullion, Brook said: 'On one condition. I want you to fathom his state of mind. He's a good fighter, one of the best. See, I wanna know if I can still count on him.' The captain sat in his armchair and threw a foot on the table. He pursued, 'He's a renegade, ain't got no place else to go, 'part from 'ere, so chances are he'll come round to our ways.'

'I am sure he won't disappoint you, Captain.'

'But I have to know if I need a vote for a new bosun or not, savvy? Before I put forward the new quartermaster . . .'

'Ah, and you intend the bosun's role for Monsieur Mattis, the former bosun of this ship.'

'Might be, you've a sharp eye.'

'Thank you, Captain, but I cannot oblige the present bosun to speak.'

'Oh, don't think I don't know it, my little Ladyship. He's a pig-headed bastard if ever there was, not unlike myself. Neither stick nor whip will bring him round, but I reckon a soft, tender touch to ease his wounds could work wonders.' The way he said it made May consider that the captain himself was not averse to a soft touch; it was why he had such affection for Joe. He pursued: 'I need to know if I've lost a good man.'

'I shall, Captain, but I am not a harlot, and I cannot peer into his soul . . . I will only see to his wound, that the stitches have not come undone, and pour alcohol over his back. For if it becomes infected, then you may as well put him out of his misery straight away.' May could hardly believe she had said that, but she must keep up her guise of aloofness.

Brook peered into her eyes. She was pretty for sure, feisty, and she painted her face subtly with an expert hand. But the question that played on his mind most was, where did she learn how to use a knife? 'Thank you, Ladyship,' said Joe. May lifted her chin and took back Joe's glass, and Brook let the question slide from his thoughts, for the time being.

*

May stepped down into the grim hold, escorted by Mossa, a big Maroon from Jamaica who May suspected of being one

110

of Brook's most loyal sailors. He was one of those who had restrained Ducamp on the captain's command, and one of the few who had given a full crack of the cat across Ducamp's bare back.

It made May shudder to think that this was where slaves were kept in chains, and where some had died of disease while she had been sleeping in a clean berth, surrounded by perfume and fine French drapery, just a dozen yards away. It was dark and dank, and it stank. She was glad she had perfumed her collar. Mossa took the large key from a hook on the wall, then unlocked the latticed iron door and entered the slave cabin. He put down the leather jug that May had asked him to carry.

Ducamp sat with his chest touching his bended knees so his back did not rub against the roughly hewn timber wall. He looked up as Mossa stepped into the cell, followed by May holding a tallow lamp and a leather bag.

Mossa cast a glance at Ducamp's blank expression, then said: 'Just holler, Me Lady, when you're done with the captain hitter!'

'Thank you,' returned May, who then strode the three yards to the bosun's large, booted feet and put down her basket as the door clunked shut behind her.

'I hear you've been a bad bosun,' she said in a lofty tone of voice.

His wounds stung as he straightened his back. He followed the length of her body with his eyes until he found her face, which he looked up at with no apparent emotion, or maybe there was a hint of defiance in his expression.

Was it one of judgement? she wondered. At least, she certainly felt partly responsible for putting thoughts into the Frenchman's head. 'Can you stand so I can check your wound?' she said with just a hint of compassion. He grunted begrudgingly while getting to his feet, but he still did not speak. In the yellow light of the tallow lamp, she inspected his stitches. The two lips of the gash seemed to have welded together already. Then she brought out a phial of rose water from her bag and poured it on a piece of sponge.

The odorous liquid was cold, but her delicate touch was soothing as she carefully explored and cleansed the wound. Her perfume had a calming effect on him as he let her hold his powerful trunk and spin him around so she could inspect his back.

'Fear not,' said Didier at last in French, which he knew Mossa could not understand. 'I am not in here because of any conversation we have had, but for my own conscience . . . and for a good man who once tried to set my thoughts straight.'

'Your father?'

'No. A better man. A Huguenot. So don't go fooling yourself into thinking you have had a bad influence over me. You are not that pretty.' He did not mean the last part, because pretty she certainly was; nobody could deny her that. No, it was more of a challenge than a statement, to see how she would react, and to perhaps distance himself from falling prey to her magnetism, her light touch, the agreeable timbre of her voice, and the shape of her body.

'Thank you, bosun,' said May, raising an eyebrow as she positioned herself behind him. 'That is reassuring to know! But you could have chosen a better time for expressing the torments of your soul! Anyway, I have not come to mourn your old self. I need an oarsman . . .'

May was not faint-hearted, but the picture before her of flayed skin, bloody welts, and hanging flesh made her take a step back and bring a hand to her mouth. Quickly recovering her composure, she then placed her hand on his shoulder as if holding a loose canvas, to steady him in case he flinched. 'Not a pretty picture,' she said caringly.

'Neither will that Mattis be once I get my hands on the bastard!'

'I believe he is after your job,' returned May, then plunged the sponge into the jug of seawater and began dowsing his back, carefully dabbing away the dried and coagulated blood.

Ducamp winced with every application of the sponge. 'God, woman!' he let out, unable to keep the pain in.

'Sorry, but it needs the sting to keep it from becoming infected.' Then, moving her mouth up to his right ear, the one further from Mossa, in a low voice she said in French: 'Now, just listen to what I have to say. As far as I can see, we are both in a fine mess, but there is a way out . . . unless you have decided to return to your old self and run with this pack of hounds?'

'No. Continue,' returned Ducamp in a half whisper.

'We are to anchor at an inlet south of Saint Augustine. Well, if you want to get out of this pickle, you are going to need an accomplice, and I happen to need an oarsman.'

'I'm listening.'

Again May touched his back with the sponge while she said: 'All I ask is that you stand ready when I come for you, once you-know-who has disembarked. Then we take the gig.'

'There'll be a gang left to manoeuvre the ship in case of danger.'

'I will deal with them.'

'And how do you . . .'

113

'Trust me. All you need to do is be ready when I come.'

'What are you going to do, bewitch them with your perfume?'

'Just trust me, and I will get you out of here. Then you help me get to Charles Town as previously agreed.'

Ducamp gave a grunt and said no more; instead, he gritted his teeth to suffer the sting of saltwater on his broken flesh. May reverted to speaking in English for the ears of Mossa when, a short time later, she said: 'There, I shall tell the captain you are still in your thoughts, and that I have mended your gash again.'

A little while later, back above deck, she told Brook that the bosun was still fuming, but she suspected he would come round eventually. Then she retired to her cabin to make preparations for their escape.

NINE

THE EVENING SKY had turned a deep red when Captain Brook gave the order to weigh anchor at the ill-famed Matanzas Inlet.

Five years ago, when he began intermittently scouring the seas on the Atlantic seaboard, the phenomenon would have surprised him, and he might have tried to figure it out. But be it the makings of the devil or God above, he still did not know, and he had long since given up trying to fathom it out. What he did know was, after a red sky at nightfall, the sea breeze that now blew softly through the rigging could whip up quick as the devil's tail and come blustering against the shoreline.

So, to avoid any misadventure while getting over the surf, he ordered the bulk of the men to take to the boats while the going was still fair. The plan was to rest under the stars ashore so they could start on their trek through thick undergrowth and wetlands upon first light. They would surprise the hell out of the township while most folk were still groggy-eyed.

'Be sure to take her out seaward on the first sign of a gale,' he said to Johnny Reed the helmsman.

'Will do, Cap'n,' returned Johnny with a firm nod.

Brook grabbed a mate's shoulder as the men began filing

over the bulwark. 'Not you, Mattis,' he said, pulling back the stocky Frenchman who, since his integration, had proven keen to please, a quality that Brook particularly valued in a new recruit. 'I want you to keep your weather eye out for our French lieutenant and the duchess. Get me?'

Brook had previously realised he had made a blunder when he had sent Mossa, who spoke no French, to escort the lady to the bosun's cell. Owing to the fact that the captain had purchased the black sailor's freedom in Jamaica, Brook knew he would follow him to hell and back and was as loyal a mate as you could get. Mossa had reported nothing untoward when May had visited Ducamp, except that they had gabbled on in French, which nevertheless for Brook raised a red flag. Why the devil would they deliberately speak in a language their gaoler did not know? Of course, it might be from sheer habit or from the woman's tendency to flaunt her refinement. But Brook was not used to giving people the benefit of the doubt, which, he assumed, was why he was still in charge of this motley crew. Besides, he had noticed that for some reason, whenever Mattis was around, May would retreat to her cabin. What did Mattis know of this lady who the late captain had taken aboard?

'Keep a close watch on her, and an ear in the hold,' he murmured to Mattis, 'or I'll have your hide proper tanned too!'

'Fear not, Captain. You can count on me,' said the French sailor eagerly as Brook climbed over the bulwark. Then Ned Brook jumped into the waiting longboat and gave the order to heave to shore.

But Mattis had his own idea, and well he knew that opportunity would not knock twice.

*

May had been busy making a draught, a powerful potion that induced deep sleep. It was similar to the mixture she had been giving to Joe, only this one had a much greater component of laudanum. In fact, she had thrown in all of the precious ingredient that she had left. But it would not work at all if she could not find a way to administer it to the remaining crew of half a dozen men.

But May was not short of foresight, and she had been planning this moment ever since the *Bella Fortuna* had been captured. Having observed the crew's customs, she had been careful to make herself a familiar sight to the men every evening when she brought her instructions to the cook for Joe's meal. In this way, she would not appear like a stranger now when she made her way to the front of the ship where the cookhouse was located.

Hammond, a large-boned and jovial character who had been given the cook's job after surviving the amputation of his right leg, even looked forward to her visits before mealtimes when she came to fill Joe's dish and cup.

'Chicken and mashed maize, Me Lady, as promised,' said the cook in his doting voice while struggling to keep his eyes from wandering below her eye line. He was not the only one to salivate at the thought of a lovely lone lady aboard, especially now with the captain gone and the bosun down in the hold. But May well knew how to slowly play on a man's desire.

'Add half an extra lemon if you will,' she returned with the authority of a woman who well knew the power of her sex appeal. She was dressed in a corset that fully covered her bust but which was close-fitting enough to fuel the imagination. 'I shall fetch his wine,' she said. While the cook went for the lemon barrel, she strode to the wine cask placed on trestles outside the kitchen cabin.

The operation of filling Joe's cup was an essential part of her plan because the grog tub was the common denominator that every man shared. She had taken care at midday to check the weight of the barrel. Had it not been heavy enough to fill everyone's cup this evening, she would have had to have found a way of running it dry for it to be changed. But she had been satisfied that there was ample left for all the remaining crew tonight. Moreover, she figured it was not due to be replaced before tomorrow, which could mean the quantity left would greatly dilute the effects of the potion. So once she had drawn off some wine for Joe, she let the wine pour into a jug to empty it further, so that the potion would be all the more potent. If anyone said anything, she would tell them she was keeping some so she would not have to keep running from one end of the ship to the other. But no one passed her; so far so good, she thought to herself, and she quickly stepped to the bulwark and threw the contents of the jug overboard. She stepped back and put the jug back down beside the barrel. Then she furtively brought out from her pocket a large vial of her special brew, which she deftly and discreetly poured through the cork hole in the top of the cask.

No one had noticed anything amiss, she was sure, not even Mattis, who she suspected had been told to keep an eye on her. But he must have gotten fed up and mooched off below, where she heard the calls and protests of men playing dominoes. But as she went to leave, she was startled by a deep voice. 'Where you off to like that, then?'

She turned around and saw the cook holding out a wooden bowl of food with cut lemons placed on the side. 'You forgot this, my lovely,' he said. 'Not so bad up there in the moon, is it, Me Lady?'

'Ah, yes, thank you, I sometimes wish I were,' she said, holding his gaze. She gave a sweet, almost saucy smile and turned in the knowledge that he would ogle her posterior, which at this moment was better than him having any suspicions as to her oversight.

Her plan was set. The men would eat their meal, drink the laced wine, and then fall asleep within the hour, leaving her free to release Ducamp and escape with her trunk in the gig. And that was as far as her planning capacity could take her, she felt. From there on the bosun would have to earn his place and come up with a plan to get them to Charles Town.

May left Joe to feed himself, then made her way back to her cabin to make final preparations. Before she had left him, he had said: 'Ladyship wants to leave the ship.'

'Wouldn't we all, Joe? Wouldn't we all,' she had returned evasively.

'I would very much, Ladyship,' he had added as she picked up her lamp, then exited the captain's cabin.

As she made her way below deck amid the dancing shadows caused by the tallow lamp, her thoughts turned to Joe's clear voice that seemed to have come out of the blue. She had been so engrossed in her escape that she had had no idea how easily he could read into her thoughts. She hoped she had not been so lax with the cook. She almost turned back to make sure Joe finished his draught, too; she could not afford any error. But then she thought she heard a creak as she approached her cabin door. The whole ship seemed to shudder from a shove broadside from an invisible force which made the timbers creak louder. She hoped the strengthening breeze would not become too blustery, and decided not to turn back and lose precious time. She paused

119

in front of her door that had been patched up since the French lieutenant put his boot through it. And it occurred to her now, what with Brook gone ashore and Ducamp locked up in a cell, that she could be considered "fair game" in this den of pirates. Thankfully, though, she had taken the precaution to tame them, and she felt they would not try it with someone they now had come to accept and, dare she say it, respect, albeit from a distance. She prayed inwardly that they would all take their wine without any exception, and that she and the bosun could get out without a hitch. Holding up the lamp to cast the maximum amount of light, she pushed the door into her room. Barely had she placed the lamp down on the dresser in front of her than she sensed a presence, the smell of rum and sweat, and then she was startled by a man's thick voice.

'Come in and shut the door,' he said. She turned briskly, hand on her collarbone, and Mattis, the former bosun, stepped forward from behind the door, which he kicked shut.

Quickly recovering her composure, she shot back a stern glare of indignation. 'What in God's name are you doing in my room?' she said in French, making her voice hard and sharp.

'Sit down and shut up,' said Mattis, defiantly nonchalant.

'I. Will. Not!'

'Suit yourself, and you can cut out the highborn lady crap with me. I know where you're from and who you are!'

A shot of alarm passed through May's mind. What did he mean? Did he know she had been in the pay of the Spanish? she wondered, but kept up her stony façade. 'How dare you speak to me like th—'

'Look, Missy, I won't beat about the bush,' returned

Mattis, looking her up and down in the mellow light of the lamp. She was a catch, and he had a smouldering fire in his loins; it was all he could do to keep himself from reaching out and squeezing her jugs. 'You oblige me with your services tonight, just this once while the lads are at play, and I'll be as mute as a map about your true colours.'

'How dare you!' May was furious as it dawned on her that her past was about to catch up with her in one way or another, and she did not want to hear about it. She craved to run away, but she could not. She could not even run out of the cabin, with Mattis standing as he was between her and the door. Her heart suddenly hardened with shame, and she mentally prepared to reach for her blade, now strapped to her arm. 'Whatever are you talking about?' she said, realising she had to find out what it was that he knew.

'Let me make myself clear, then, shall I? See, I was the one who hooked your whoring robe when you threw it through the window, not Reners. And I was standing behind the door when you owned up you were a courtesan, which, correct me if I'm wrong, is posh talk for whore. Don't try to deny it.'

'You are mad, Mattis, and you have been drinking! You have no proof of what you advance. You are just trying it on because Captain Reners is not here to defend my honour!'

'Then it'll be your word against mine when I tell Captain Brook, won't it, Ladyship!' he said, punctuating his words with a mocking laugh.

May was outraged. She almost hoped he would attack her now so she would have a pretext to defend her honour with her blade. But though she had sliced a man before, she had never killed one, or plunged a knife in a man's belly. The thought of it made her cringe, but she knew she was capable of anything to get to Charles Town, to get to her treasure. But she sensed he was not about to try to take her. It was through blackmail that he wanted to have her, something more dastardly that excited him more, no doubt; something he could brag about. However, the obnoxious little imp had a point, and she still had her robes hidden away in her trunk, her favourite one and the crimson one that Captain Reners had brought back to her. It would not take much to force the lock. She was outraged and cornered. If Brook ever found out about her past, she would be like a fox thrown to a pack of hounds. Throughout her life, she had often been cornered; it was nothing new, though until now, it had been through lack of means. And owing to her good looks, and her bearing, she had always been able to choose the least dishonourable path, which was why she had chosen the life of a courtesan. The least soul-destroying route to get to the place she wanted to be, a place in the north where she could turn over a new leaf as a woman of means.

So she forced herself to rekindle that persona she had created, the character she had hoped would never rear its head again. She arched her back, relaxed her hips, and placed her left elbow on her dagger hand, and nonchalantly framed her pretty face with her left ring and index fingers. She offered a smile at the grubby man opposite, whose sweat stank to high heaven of rum, no doubt to prick up his courage. Yet he had not attempted to snatch her, so she surmised that, in his new piratical role that must have gone to his head, he was either being naively optimistic that she would concede, or he was in awe of her. Either way, she well knew how men like Mattis functioned when they did not get what they wanted. He was a counter-puncher, whose lack of self-confidence would lead him to fear she was looking down on him. Then he would force himself upon her and beat her to cover up his frustration, unless of course she planted a knife in his belly. But that would be a mess, and besides, her blade was still attached to her forearm. No, there was a cleaner way out of this if she wanted to escape this godforsaken ship. If she was ever to make it back to Charles Town to pick up her little treasure and find that new life further north. 'All right, pirate Mattis,' she said, enticing and yet dignified, 'only once will you see me in *uniform.*' Then, pushing him gently backwards to the doorway by the tips of her fingers, coquettishly, she said: 'But first, you must wait outside for me to change.' She then opened the door and pushed him out.

How easily men could become devoid of all intellect when their lust was held hostage, she thought to herself as she dug into her trunk for a change of clothes. May changed quickly, not into her beautiful gown made for a governor's courtesan, but into the outfit she had prepared for her nightly caper. Then she pulled out a length of cord that she had previously prepared for Captain Reners in case he had tried to enter her room during the night. She attached one end at ankle height to a nail in the timber wall, to the right of the door as the walker went in, and wrapped the other to a leg of her berth so that the string ran taut two yards in front of her chair that faced the door.

Meanwhile, Mattis had already primed himself for the party ahead and was becoming impatient. 'What you up to in there?' he said in a low voice, his forehead touching the timber door. He did not want to alert the other lascars of his antics; they would only get jealous and spoil everything. 'I'm coming in!'

'Then enter, my prince!' said May in a lubricious voice, suffixing her words in her mind with *of fools*.

The prince of fools in question burst in through the door, a lascivious curl upon his lip which turned sour the moment he saw his pretty prize sitting in the chair opposite, bathed in the yellow light from the dimmed lamp. 'Where's your finery?' he said, feeling let down.

She was wearing thigh boots, breeches, and a shirt teasingly unbuttoned so that it revealed the generous cleft of her bust. She stamped a heel on the floor and got enticingly to her feet, arching her back and pushing against her thighs as she did so. She said: 'Come on in, then, sailor. Show me what big hands you have.' Mattis's grin flashed across his face again as he stepped toward the object of his desire.

A belaying pin was a hardwood peg a foot long and used to secure lines to the inner bulwark. The peg end was straight where it fit into the hole. The other end, around which the rope was looped, was bulbous, and perfect as a handle if used as a club. And May was holding one up her baggy sleeve.

It was not hard to keep the sailor's eyes directed at her. No sooner had he taken two steps forward than he tripped on the cord that May had attached from behind the door to the berth leg at ankle height. He went hurtling to the ground under his own momentum. As he did so, May swiftly brought out her improvised cosh and thwacked the sailor on the side of his large head. His initial cry fell into a low grunt as he hit the ground, face down in a state of unconsciousness. May soon had her left knee firmly planted in the small of his back as she stuffed a rag into his mouth. Then she quickly proceeded to bind his wrists behind his back, and then his ankles, which she managed to pull up to his wrist ties.

'There, that's just how I imaged you, a worm!' she jeered, standing over the body before quickly returning to her preparations.

'Right, all I need now is a hunk to haul this little lot into the gig,' she said to herself, looking at her trunk, her inward eye on the French lieutenant who had stupidly gotten himself flogged and who was presently locked up in the hold. But when all was said and done, it was perhaps a blessing in disguise, she thought, for at least, it meant he had not gone ashore with the invading party.

An hour later, the distant noise of cheering was replaced by the rumbling snorts of sleep. May looked down at the sailor still lying unconscious on the floor and wondered if she ought to unbind his hands so that he could at least save himself in case the ship got into difficulties later. For the *Bella Fortuna* was now rolling at anchor, as the dark night brought with it sudden flurries of wind that now and again slammed against the broadside, making the vessel tilt. If it became stormy, Mattis would have no way of saving his rotten hide if he were bound hands and feet. There came a grunt from his person while she inspected his ties. Her life would be at stake if he came round while she was still aboard, and May was a survivor. So she decided to let him be and sheathed her knife before making her way to the main deck.

*

The hold was pitch-dark. No one had come to light a lamp, and Didier could hardly see his hands before his eyes.

An hour earlier, he heard the men clomping about on the gun deck above, hollering cheerful insults and giving back chaff. Now, however, even though the wind had picked up, all he could hear through the ship's timbers was the rolling of objects and the deep rumbling of snoring sailors. Yet he knew, as they all did, about the reputation of the inlet with its narrow channels and shifting sandbars. If they did not

125

react in time, the *Bella Fortuna* could be pushed, her anchor dragged, and become caught on a sandbar with the retreating tide.

'Ahoy there!' he yelled out again. 'Wake up, you daft bastards!'

At length, he saw the glow of a lamp as at last someone descended into the hold, then stood at the foot of the steps as if in contemplation. 'What you bloody waiting for, man?' growled Ducamp to the stranger who was visibly looking around the deck. 'What you after?'

'I am looking for the keys, so shut your bone box!' said a voice harshly in a hoarse whisper, but with none of the coarseness of the usual mate.

'Oh, it's you!' said Didier, in a more subdued though nonetheless surprised tone of voice. The lady was astonishingly resourceful, he thought to himself as he wagged a finger between the iron slats. 'On a hook to the right of the door.'

As she unlocked his prison door, May explained in a few words how she had administered her sedative to the crew and knocked out Mattis. They made their way to the gun deck, where mates were slumped over tables or cradled in hammocks, and continued above, where they were met by intermittent squalls and the rushing sound of the retreating sea. The outgoing current and the contrary wind were probably what kept the ship from dragging her anchor, thought Ducamp, but how deep was the water beneath them now? he wondered.

The main deck was deserted, and dim and eerie as a ghost ship. Nevertheless, Ducamp half crouched in case anyone came prowling as he went for the plumb line that was kept midship.

'Wait, where are you going?' cried out May, to make

herself heard above the wind howling through the rigging. 'There's my trunk to bring up from my cabin!'

'There's things more urgent than ladies' garments!' returned Ducamp.

'The tide is going out. She might get stuck, but she won't be broken till the tide returns. By then, the crew will have woken.'

The lady did have a point. 'But she'll be grounded,' returned Ducamp. 'In a big sea, she'll still be smashed on the seabed come morning.'

'So what!' said May; then she made to go astern. 'Come on. It contains treasure and plate from the captain's cabin!'

Despite his niggles of the soul, he had never forgotten that he had joined the crew on the promise of a quick fortune, so he was not insensitive to the mention of treasure; which was, after all, the essential ingredient for a man's earthly freedom, and one which no doubt made fearing God a lot simpler. Clad as she was, she cut a different figure from the perfect lady he first met, he thought as he moved swiftly to catch up with her. This was evidently a woman of means. And she was right about what she said should the ship be left on a sandbar. The water would retract, then rise up with the next incoming tide to float her again. On the other hand, if the weather turned rough, the *Bella Fortuna* could well be lifted and dumped time and again upon the seabed until her hull split. He cast his eyes shoreward to the glowing embers of a beach fire. It was the fire of the pirates who at dawn would raid the Spanish township. No, the death of these desperados would be no loss to the world, he thought as he followed her down into her quarters.

May stood on the threshold of the cabin, seeing an empty space where she had left Mattis bound and unconscious.

'What's wrong?' said Ducamp as he arrived a moment later.

'Nothing, just making sure everything's still here.' Ducamp followed her gaze to the opposite side, where Mattis, lying bound and inert, must have slid with the pitch of the ship.

'Nice work,' said Ducamp with a whistle of appreciation; then he took the opposite end of May's large trunk. 'Christ, what did you say was inside?' said Ducamp, grabbing a handle of the trunk to feel the weight.

'The captain's silver, some plate, and never you mind the rest . . .'

They heaved the trunk half a dozen steps at a time, so May could recover her strength and adjust her grip on the handle. Then they mounted the steps to the main deck, two steps at a time.

Half an hour later, having lowered the gig over the leeward gunwale, Ducamp said: 'It's too heavy. If we let go from the bulwark, it'll go straight through the gig. We'll need to winch it over the—' But before he could finish his sentence, there came a loud blast, followed by the thud of lead shot sinking into the wood of the bulwark. Ducamp and May shot a glance back across the deck.

'And where you think you're going?' said the voice of Mattis, who materialised out of the darkness and swaggered across the deck. He let drop the discharged flintlock to the floor and took another from his belt. Now standing his ground behind his two remaining pistols, one aimed at May and the other at Ducamp, he said: 'I've two shots, and they won't miss their target, so put that down, and get your butts into the hold!'

Neither Ducamp nor May made a move at first, stunned

as they were to see the man who, a short while earlier, they had seen lying inert on the floor of May's cabin. 'NOW!' he hurled, which shook the would-be escapees from their stupor. 'Ha, surprised to see me, eh, Missy?' he said as he ushered them toward the hatchway. 'Painted ladies shouldn't leave their personal accessories lying around, because nail files can come in very handy when your hands are tied. We'll soon see what Captain Brook has to say about this little conspiracy to wreck his ship . . . and that ain't all, is—'

Mattis did not close his sentence. Instead, May and Ducamp heard a loud crack like wood on wood, followed by a sound like that of a heavy sack dropping to the floor. They turned in unison to find Mattis collapsed in a heap at their feet, and two wide eyes above a white beaming smile where the matelot had stood.

'Joe?' exclaimed May, hand on her waist. She immediately noticed the object that had caused Mattis to fall a second time this evening. Joe was holding a belaying pin, though this one was longer than May's. She deduced that Joe must have used both hands to swing it with such force.

'Can I come too?' he said.

*

May sat up on her trunk in the middle of the boat, trying to peer above the sea at the embers on the dark shore. Raising her voice above another flurry of wind, she said: 'Surely we risk being seen if we run straight to shore.'

Ducamp was facing her, pulling at the oars. 'It'll be a battle against wind and tide if we don't!' he said, nodding seaward where there was another series of lightning flashes. 'Best not stay on the water with a storm on its way.'

Joe, who was rowing behind her at the aft, twisted his linen-clad torso around and said: 'There's another bay southward.'

'How do you know, Joe?' returned May, throwing her voice over her shoulder.

'I bin here before, Ladyship. It's where we used to catch the green turtle.'

The wind by now was whipping up the water and intermittently sending cold spray onto the oarsmen's backs and May's face.

'Joe's right,' said Ducamp. 'The captain will be heading northward, so we'll just have to row against the current to the next inlet down.'

May nodded in agreement and said: 'Pity we haven't a mast.'

Half an hour later, they had rowed far enough south against the current and were putting in to shore, which lay barely thirty yards ahead. But with the land breeze against them and the tide having turned, the retreating current was steadily growing stronger and pushing the light gig backwards, cancelling the progress made by the rowers. 'We'll never make it ashore at this rate!' blurted out Ducamp as thunder boomed in the near distance. His back was stinging from his wounds, made more painful by the effort and the salty sea. Again they heaved; again their progress was wiped out by the strong reversing current. Unable to just sit there, May spun around on the trunk to reposition herself with her legs on either side of Joe, who had his back to her. She reached for the oars in an attempt to lend extra heaving power.

But amid the rush of the wind and the wash of the sea, she suddenly felt the oars become heavier as Joe let go of them, saying: 'Keep rowing, Lady, I push the boat in the sea.'

'No!' cried May, 'you'll drown!'

'Fear not, Ladyship,' said Joe cheerfully. Then he slipped overboard before either Didier or May could utter another word to prevent him. A moment later, his head bobbed up in the swelling sea, and then, placing his hands on the stern rim, he beat his feet in the water to help propel the boat forward, while Didier and May rowed in unison with all their might. The extra propulsion was enough to get them beyond the sandbanks between which the strong reversing current had formed.

Ten minutes later, bone-tired, they dragged the little boat up the compact foreshore, past the sea debris of the tide line. Once they had turned the boat over on top of the trunk, Joe scrambled up a palm tree to chop down some of its wide leaves, while Ducamp went scouring the area for robust fallen branches to make a lean-to against the draught. Behind the boat, where the beach met the first sprinkling of trees, May proceeded to build a fire from kindling she recovered nearby.

By the time Ducamp returned from scouring the dark shoreline for extra debris and dead wood, he was heartened and surprised to see the small fire neatly made, the boat screening its light from the north. For some reason, it always intrigued him when a woman made a fire, and he decided there was definitely more to this lady than met the eye, for even he would have been hard put to kindle a flame in this weather. 'Well, well,' he said with a laugh in his voice. 'How did you do that?'

'Do you doubt my resourcefulness, Lieutenant?'

'No, no, that's not what I meant,' he replied, letting the wood fall from his cradled arms as a sense of guilt trickled through his conscience. 'I mean, it ain't easy finding the

131

right wood, let alone rubbing them till they smoke.'

'I know, Lieutenant,' said May. 'That is why I brought a flint and steel!' This lady had everything sorted, thought Didier, lost for a moment in admiration. 'Joe,' she called out in a hoarse whisper, 'that's enough leaves. Come down and warm yourself by the fire before you catch your death!'

'Coming, Ladyship!' said Joe, who then scooted down the smooth tree trunk.

The lady certainly had a way with folk, thought Ducamp, neither too snappy nor too gentle. She knew her mind. He put together a rudimentary frame for a lean-to while Joe and May laid down the palm leaves to sleep on. The remaining leaves went to form a canopy to give shelter till the break of day.

They drank from a gourd and ate dried meat and lentils. 'Now what do we do?' said May a little while later, having returned from a call of nature. 'I doubt the gig is enough to get us to Charles Town.'

During her absence, Ducamp had been turning their options over in his mind, for now it was his turn to provide. 'No, it would be hard enough to break the surf, even.'

'There's a river,' said Joe, sitting bare-chested, his shirt stretched out on the boat near the fire.

'That's right,' said Ducamp, 'runs along the coast further in. It's not far; I saw it while looking for wood. But it must lead to Saint Augustine. Not the best time to make an appearance . . .'

'We could pretend you're my manservant,' said May.

Ducamp flashed her a dubious look before Joe jumped in. 'Before it reaches the town,' he said, 'there's a fork in the river. The right fork leads into the harbour, but the left one goes around the back of the town.'

'Captain's sure lost a treasure losing you, man,' said Ducamp, slapping the mulatto on the shoulder in a comradely way.

The land breeze kept the storm at bay, and they slept without rainfall until morning light. Despite the discomfort of sleeping on his belly, Didier was relieved to be free from the grips of piracy, and in the company of May and little Joe—Joe whom he realised must have played along with Brook through hope of escape. It was clear to him now that the little mulatto had not enjoyed but rather endured Brook's company.

TEN

NED BROOK HAD that pre-battle feeling, the one that in him combined fear, hunger, and lust.

What if the ship did not make it into the bar-bound roadstead, flying Spanish colours? Then what? The Spanish soldiers would not come filing out of the fort to defend the harbour. He and his men would not be able to take the partially defended fort from the west. 'But in that case,' he thought to himself, 'I'll send a party to set fire to bloody houses in the east to create my diversion, and still attack the fort from the west as planned.'

Brook was contented with his plan B and quashed any further what-ifs; he had no time for them. He had no time for anything much other than making his mark on this world of thieves. The thieves who took from the natives, the upper crust who thieved from the lower classes and kept them in poverty, the English who thieved from the French, and the French who thieved from everyone. It was all a bloody macabre dance of thieves: this New World was a thieves' party. And this raid would make him one of the biggest thieves of them all, a dark prince of desperados. It would go down in history. Not epic like Morgan's raid on

Panama, but quick and simple, and just as rewarding. Then he would disappear, and live out his days with Joe in Virginia or in the great plains of the north where the buffalo roamed.

Lucky the moon was covered over, he thought as he turned to the east where the *Bella Fortuna* was engulfed by the night; the blanket of darkness would last all the longer. He could hardly make out the first white crests of the waves, let alone the ship. The offshore storm had ceased to blow, for there were no more flashes of lightning on the sea. They must have extinguished the ship's lanterns, and rightly so, he thought. Otherwise, any shore dweller might see her and jeopardize her slipping into the Saint Augustine roadstead in the guise of a Spanish merchantman. If she set off in the morning twilight, she would easily reach the roadstead by the first rays of sunlight.

He wondered what he was going to do with that idiot Ducamp. If the man did not come round and see sense soon, then he would lose a good bosun, he thought to himself. It was always a letdown when one of his young lieutenants got killed through lack of killer instinct or through a waning pleasure for the fight. Ducamp had been a professional soldier; he did it because it was his job, not through passion, like Brook. Ned Brook loved the thrill of the fight, the melee and the coup de grace. He was a natural predator, and he administered the final blow without remorse.

'Come on, lads!' he growled in a low voice, and his hand motioned to the boats waiting on the riverbank that ran parallel to the shoreline. 'We wanna get positioned well before the first breath of day.'

The company of fifty-five men, goaded by their mutual desperation to make good in this life through this one life-changing raid, filled the three boats in silence, except for the odd grunt and chesty cough. Brook sat at the stern in the first of them. He would keep an eye out for the first lights of lanterns as night began to pale and the folk began to stir to the new day. This was the part he loved: the stalking, the stealth, the camaraderie in battle. Then would come the surprise attack, the killing, and the final prize.

The first time Ned Brook killed a man was when he was thirteen. He did it because a desperate outlaw broke into his father's old cobbler workshop. The lad had taken up his dad's hunting musket and held the culprit at the end of the barrel. A thirteen-year-old boy, suddenly all powerful, and a thirty-year-old man with grovelling eyes. Brook could never forget that immense feeling of power. Then it had occurred to the boy that the man was in the wrong, that he was just a boy, and that a musket could go off by accident. He had often killed kittens and had always wondered what it was like to kill a man. And there he was, his finger itching to pull the trigger, just once. So he took aim, smiled at the man, and shot him between the eyes. It was both horrible and fascinating to see a man's brain cracked open like a walnut. He had felt bewildered, and then his dad came bursting in, followed by neighbours, who all congratulated him for killing the outlaw who had also visited their food stores at some point. He had committed his first murder, and he would get away with it. Now that he knew he could do it he felt relieved, like a girl who tried whoring for the first time and successfully drew pleasure.

The next time it happened was one blowy day when walking along the Beer Hill clifftop, bagging snared rabbits. He had been with his uncle Hamlin, the one who had buggered him. He had set a snare near the cliff edge. Silly thing to do, really, but it had worked. Because of the wind, his uncle took the initiative to retrieve the rabbit. Ned was a big lad already, and as his uncle stood up, he gave him a good, powerful shove. The surprised uncle went clean over but just managed to grasp onto a grassy tuft of the limestone ledge.

'Give me your hand,' his uncle had commanded angrily. But Ned just stood there watching. The uncle became wary, and fear suddenly filled his eyes as the boy drew closer, with a rock held tightly in his fist.

'Ned, no, wait!'

The lad, with a mad light in his eye and a sly smile on his lips, lowered to his knees. How Hamlin had screamed in pain and frustration as Ned methodically set about smashing his uncle's fingers one by one. 'You'll be dead in a few seconds, Uncle Hamlin,' he said gleefully before the final blow. Then the lad watched the man drop with a terrified cry which ceased a few seconds later. There would be no reprisal, and no man would ever hold any ascendance over Ned Brook again. He had no remorse, and his problem was simply gone.

No, not everyone was like Ned Brook; not everyone had that killer instinct. It took some time before Ned himself realised he was quite exceptional, and that very few men had that true killer instinct. He used to wonder if he would go to hell, but then he stopped thinking about it. He knew now that even the hardiest of pirates ended up having regrets and remorse. The trick was to squeeze as much out of them while they were still keen. Besides, killing was as natural in God's world as giving birth. Take the alligator or the wolf. Did it have remorse when it took a calf at the water's edge or a lamb at the edge of a flock? Of course not, it was the natural way of things. A natural order and he was at the top. All he

137

needed now was a proper hoard of silver.

The boats followed the fork in the river. The right fork carried on to the natural harbour east of the port town; the left fork would take them behind the settlement. Brook now saw the first lamplights come alive. These were the early birds who lived on the land outside the port town and provided provisions. A few furlongs later, he was surprised to see that the settlement had become a cosy little township, and they were now putting up stone houses, no less.

Ten minutes later, the three boats were being hauled up the grassy shore of the brackish river where the horde of rovers crouched in the undergrowth around their leader.

'Remember, lads,' said Brook in his low, deep voice, 'on the first cannon fire, we take out the sentries. Rob, Jimmy, you plant the bombs at the doors. Roger and Paulo, you stand ready with axes to finish them off!'

The fort was being built north of the town, opposite a spit of land where the eastside river turned into the estuary. The east walls looked directly onto this estuary, facing any would-be aggressors from the sea before they hit the township. The south side, where the entrance was situated, faced the township. The band of pirates hacked through the woodland from the west, where the land was still wild. At the edge of a thicket, Brook could hardly believe his eyes. The hardest bit would be to sneak up close to the fort to carry out their plan. But lo and behold, the idiots had cultivated the fields all around this side of the fort. It meant the men were able to approach the west wall under cover of maize stalks taller than man height. Brook felt relieved; his plan was going even better than expected. Nevertheless, he was careful not to call victory, because it often happened that when things started off smoothly, they ended up in chaos.

They had made good time. As the dawn began to pale, they advanced between the clumps of maize. They crouched near the edge of the field along the north road that must lead to the country, and waited for sunrise and the first blasts of cannons.

*

Sam was peeing against a tree in the paling grey light.

He worked at the quarry on Anastasia Island, the spit of land opposite the main settlement. This was where squares of coquina were extracted for the stonecutters to then chop into shape for the masons. Once extracted, the shell stone was loaded onto carefully balanced rafts and ferried across to the building site north of the township.

But in the early morning, he loved to fish at a creek near the fork of the saline river, where he could catch the great sea trout. The biggest he had caught this year was three feet long and had brought in a tidy sum. But that was back in the spring, and now the fish were smaller, but still worth getting up for. *Worth getting up for, there's a phrase*, he thought to himself as he passed it back through his mind in Spanish, while shaking himself at the tree. Only two years earlier, he had escaped the English colony of Charles Town with seven other slaves and three children who, in accordance with the Spanish policy to take in runaway slaves from the British colony, were given refuge by the Spanish governor Diego de Quiroga y Losada. The men were given work on the quarry for a salary, and the women served in the governor's house.

Sam was not averse to hard work. In fact, he worked well and found he was more suited to it than the local Timucua Indians who dropped like flies whenever there was distemper in the air. He was strong and resistant and had moved up in status to become a stonecutter, which meant he could double his pay, a far cry from the days of slavery in the English colony. For nothing in the world would he give it up, and there was still plenty of work yet, cutting coquina for the fort on the other side of the estuary. He had learnt Spanish, converted to Catholicism, and had become an integral part of Saint Augustine society.

As he turned back to the marshy creek, Sam thought he saw something on the river crossing the water into the left fork. Probably a bull gator on the prowl, he thought to himself as he instinctively looked around him at his feet in the half light. For it was that time of year when the young hatched, and a mother could get vicious if she sensed a threat. Having assured himself there were no gators big or small nearby, he looked again across the water. He kept still to accustom his eyes to the backdrop of the river vegetation and realised that what he had seen was much too long to be a bull. Or could it be a giant beast? But as the thought entered his mind, so did the sound of hushed voices. He grew wary, for he could swear he heard words in English about mosquitoes biting everywhere.

Sam backed into the undergrowth as the three boats slipped through the water on the far side. He knew who these people were. They were rovers come to ransack the town, like the ones who had come last year. Sam did not want the town to be ruined: it was his town, his home now. He backed away slowly, then ran back to the landing stage where the blocks of shell stone were ferried. But at this hour, there was no one to work the rope ferry. Besides, if any of the pirates came this way, they would see him, and he would be a sitting duck. He was a good swimmer, having learnt to do so when in Africa as a boy. But the alligators were rife in these parts, and not only that, it was hatching season; the mothers could become snappy. However, his home was worth defending.

He bundled up his breeches and shirt and tied them around his neck so they could sit on his shoulders. Then he slowly slipped into the cool water, his eating knife between his teeth. He was two-thirds of the way to the opposite bank when a movement, a splash from the bushes behind him, made him turn his head in mid-stroke.

An alligator. A bull.

He turned into another stroke and propelled himself with his feet under the water as the gator came sliding swiftly in his wake. He knew gators had no interest in humans, but him being in the water, the alligator would not think twice. He was prey like any other in the reptile's dark, watery kingdom.

But Sam did not think he was going to die in the water, for he had a mission, and he had been taught that God was on the side of the righteous. A few minutes later, he was scrambling up the bank as the gator came snapping, its jaws three yards behind him.

He jumped into his breeches and pulled on his coarse cotton shirt. Then he hurried along the shore of the bay and through the streets of the township, dodging heaps of hewn stone and scaffolding that emerged from the greyness as he approached. These were the blocks of stone the governor had decided to allow townsfolk to purchase so they could build stronger stone houses to replace their wattle and daub dwellings. Sam's first reflex was to run to the governor's house, where his wife worked.

*

141

Listening to Sam in the candle-lit hallway of his residence made of stone, Diego de Quiroga y Losada knew what the thieves had come for. He knew the silver was bound to attract a villainous visit once word had gotten out.

He had been in the settlement for three years. He had learnt about the ways of the colonists and had voiced their grievances to the crown. Most of all, he had secured the means to continue with the last stages of the fort.

The settlement had been attacked by pirates in the past, and the raiders had been defeated. But this time, he did not order the alarm bell to be rung. This time, he would let them come to him. Besides, it was already too late to stage a defence strategy, and these pirates would be determined to lay their hands on the hoard of silver that lay in store in the unfinished fort.

'I want you to spread word. Go swiftly and quietly,' he said to Sam and his three male servants. 'Tell everyone, if they bar their doors and batten their shutters, there is a good chance they won't be visited, for these thieves have greater aspirations on their mind.'

Sam and the men divided themselves up and went about their task, rapping on doors and whispering through the locks.

Then Diego hurried to the fort to alert Captain Ayala. The captain said: 'Coming up the river, you say? Then we should dispatch men on the bank and pick them off as they approach.'

'We don't know where they are, or how many; we might be attacked from both sides,' said the governor. 'No, I have a better plan. We let them come knocking at our door, and we let them in…'

'But they will burn down the town.'

'A pirate's greed is far greater than his vice of destruction. They will head straight for the silver.'

'I don't like it. These bastards are like rats: they get in where you least expect it. And may I remind you, Governor, the corn is now high around the fort. It will give them cover almost right up to our walls, walls that are unfinished. I told you it was dangerous to plant around the fort.'

'The people have to eat, Captain.'

'That is so, but these men are wild desperados. They have no mercy. They kill indiscriminately.'

'They are after the silver. They will know where it is guarded. They will not risk alerting the garrison before their assault.' The captain winced in disagreement.

*

Brook shook his men into action at the crack of dawn.

He had been thinking of the reputation he would earn with the acquisition of the salvaged Spanish silver. The Spaniards would not expect a raid from the south, let alone from the west, and their big guns would be turned toward the sea entrance. By first light, the rovers had navigated up the meandering channel of the tidal river that ran west of the town. Then they had beached their rowboats on the muddy bank. Now they were crouching in the maize field on the edge of the path that led out of town northward. They waited for the boom of cannon fire to give them the cue to attack.

The first sunbeams cracked through the clouds. Still no sign of the *Bella Fortuna,* which was supposed to deliver the diversion before sailing back out to sea.

Another half hour went by. Brook could curse the beggars. All they had to do was enter the roadstead, make a

143

noise, and sail out. After another half hour, the sun was full up. He figured they must have missed the tide, and he would lose the element of surprise if he did not act quickly. He turned to Mossa and began to tell him to trigger plan B. He would take three men and find a fire in town, then quickly set light to thatching along the east side to draw out the soldiers, for climbing the fort walls was not an option. Though the fort was not yet finished, it still constituted a strong place. Mossa was about to select his acolytes when there came the rattling sound of a cart drawn by a donkey. Brook motioned to Mossa to hold it. All they had to do was surprise the Spanish bastards, he thought to himself. They just needed to open that gate, and Brook now realised they could do so through stealth. He turned to his main men and quickly whispered the new plan of attack. Then, nodding toward the carter rolling in from the north twenty yards up, he said: 'Take 'im, and don't let him squeal!'

*

Juano Mantello lived off the land, which he had worked hard to turn into a prairie to the north of the settlement.

That was the side which, over the years, had proven to be the most tranquil, despite the odd raid from British soldiers and Yamasee Indians who sailed down from Carolina. For the back door into Saint Augustine was to the south.

Juano supplied the settlement with fresh milk and salt, and every day, he rode into town to earn his crust. Before setting off, while putting on his boots, he had told his wife that he must trade some salt for a leg of ham. He had meant to do it yesterday, but his wife, Puri, had accompanied him into town to visit their daughter, who had married a fisherman, and they had stayed to chatter too long. For his daughter had announced that she was pregnant again, so Juano had ridden back without his ham. But Juano loved ham; it reminded him of his life as a boy in his home village near Badajoz, where the black pigs roamed the evergreen oak forests and fed solely on acorns in summer.

But before riding into town, as usual he would pass by the fort, his best customer, to deliver his daily urn of milk. The sun was already beaming through the clouds, warming the ground from a night of stormy weather as the fort came into view. 'Easy, boy,' he said to his donkey, who had pricked its ears and then come to a halt. 'Come on, you stupid beast,' he said and gave it a light swipe with his stick. 'The way is clear, you silly old ass. Alligators don't eat donkeys. I've told you before!' He touched the animal again with his stick. It pulled its head and reluctantly walked on.

Juano caught a movement in the corner of his eye. As he turned his head to see, he felt a large hand grasp his mouth and drag him off the cart. He tried to elbow his assailant, but the hand was strong and covered his face and mouth so that he could neither breathe nor scream his utter fear. He could only turn his eyes to the bloody sunrise as he felt a sharp blade slide swiftly across his throat.

*

'I didn't tell you to kill the man!' said Brook as Mossa pulled up in the cart by the maize field that lined the road.

'You told me not to let him squeal, Captain,' said Mossa in all innocence. They were barely fifty yards from the fort. Luckily, an old leafy tree covered them from view.

'Take his jacket and hat and throw him in the bushes, a gator'll soon sniff 'im out,' said Brook. Then, turning to a short-limbed, olive-skinned sailor beside him, he said:

'Right, Pedro, put on his coat, and ride up to the gate. And remember to stall the cart on the threshold so we can get in, savvy?'

*

The governor had not thought of the possibility that the men in the boat could have been Indians, and more and more, it was looking likely that they were.

He was standing with Captain Ayala on the ledge behind the great south wall in construction.

Ayala was beginning to regret that he had foolishly let himself be persuaded by the governor to let the pirates wander clean into the fort, should they show themselves. He told himself he would not succumb again. For what sane commander would let a horde of cutthroats seize the very stronghold that was built to save their lives?

But Governor Diego de Quiroga y Losada was mindful of the wellbeing of the population. 'You know what will happen if we let these villains take the town, Captain. They will hold the townspeople hostage until they find a way of entering the fort—the fort, need I remind you, that is not yet finished.' Then he had cooked up a plan to let the bandits inside in order to contain them.

Past dawn and still no sign of the rascals, thought the governor. A minute later, word was passed along the west wall that the cart of the milkman was on its way, like every day except on the Lord's Day.

The captain gave a fatigued look at the governor standing beside him. 'Check there are no pirates hiding in the urns!' he said with a hint of irony.

A little while later, the cart was tranquilly rolling toward the south-facing gate, and the sky had grown perceptibly lighter. Clad in Juano's blue jacket, Pedro raised a hand and dipped his wide-brimmed hat to the sentry atop the watchtower.

'It's Juano, come to invade us!' said the sentry to the guard below him. Then the heavy timber gate creaked open.

'*Hola*, Juano,' hailed the guard, casting a rapid eye inside the cart, where there were just some urns and a sack of salt. A second later, he registered the youth of the man's hands holding the reins of the donkey.

No one of the garrison could be sure of an imminent attack; it had been discussed that the boats Sam had seen could have been Indians rowing around the township under the cover of night. It was a common enough occurrence and was tolerated, provided they went on their way to the northern territories. Who would be stupid enough to attack a fort, albeit one in construction?

The guard suddenly realised his wishful thinking had tricked him, and the nervous realisation flashed in his eyes. But before he could utter another word, a black hand smothered his nose and mouth while a razor-sharp knife was pulled across his throat. At the same time, the sentinel was taken out by a flying dagger.

Pedro advanced the cart so it blocked the gate. Then he jumped down as Jack and Barry went to set down grenades to blow up the inner gate. But they quickly discovered that the unfinished gate was already half open. 'We're in, lads!' Barry blurted out. There came a terrifying uproar from fifty treasure-hungry cutthroats as they stormed the entrance from the edge of the cornfield.

Ned Brook and a few other crack shots hung back to pick off any adversaries who showed their heads above the parapet. But no one did, so they soon joined the surge to get through to the courtyard, where Brook imagined the waking garrison had not had time to sound the alarm. This would be a lightning attack, and Brook knew what to head for. But once in through the gates, a terrible thought chilled his blood. There were no guns, the gate was child's play to get through and, judging from the lads trying to kick their way into the fort buildings, all the doors must have been locked before they arrived. 'Out! Get the hell out, lads!' he blustered as he backed into the gateway, brandishing his pistols. 'It's a bloody trap!'

But as he bundled through the gate with Mossa and a handful of other pirates, there came a cracking volley of gunfire as, inside the fort quadrangle, the invaders were being shot dead by garrison soldiers who now showed themselves, taking aim with their muskets, along the parapets.

Brook's group huddled behind the cart for cover. If only they could use it as a shield to get to the edge of the cornfield, they might stand a chance. But they had to act quickly while the lookout soldiers were turned toward the massacre taking place in the courtyard.

'Turn the donkey round,' blasted Brook. His orders were carried out. The donkey was backed out of the porch gateway and Pedro's milk cart with it.

But as Brook and his men kept up fire while walking behind the cart, the Spaniards shot at the beast, who crumpled to the ground under a volley of lead. They had nonetheless managed to travel half the distance to the cornfield. They could make a dash for it, but every man knew they would not all make it alive. Brook, as sharp on his feet as ever, said: 'Jack, Roger, cut the straps away. We'll bloody well push it.'

Jack and Roger, who both knew there was no place safer

than beside ole Brook when in battle, crept under the cart and cut free the binds that still held the donkey to the two shafts. Now they could push the cart clean over the dead beast.

'Jack, Rog, push the bloody thing from the rear!' ordered Brook.

'We'll get shot, Cap'n!' said Jack.

'Nah, you'll be all right, man. We'll cover your filthy hides . . . Now get shoving, mates!'

A moment later, the two men were heaving the cart forward while Brook and the others gave them fire cover. But it was not long before the pistols needed reloading, and when their fire ceased, Brook yelled out: 'Come on, you lascars! A few more lengths! Come on, push the bloody thing! Push!' But the instant he blurted out his command, there came a well-aimed barrage that this time sank into the backs and the skulls of the two pushers.

'Come 'ere, Trev. While they're reloading... Can't stay 'ere, or we're sitting ducks. This way!' hurled Brook, grabbing one of the young pirates by the shirt and steering him toward the cornfield.

'I'll get shot, Cap'n,' cried Trevor.

'You'll be all right, lad. Just stay with me, and don't stop!' Brook ran on the inside of Trevor while clasping the mate's left arm.

'Ahh! I'm hit!' cried Trevor when the first shots came whistling through the air.

'Just keep moving, lad!' hurled Brook, who now was clasping the man's shirt under his jacket and pulling him along. But the human shield went limp and was soon too heavy to drag. Nevertheless, Brook had made it to the cornfield with Mossa. They lost no time in dashing through the lacerating leaves that cut any visible flesh, hands, cheeks . . .

'The boat's ahead, Cap'n,' called Mossa, who beat through the thicket to the riverside.

'Cut it loose, ready to kick her off,' returned Brook, whose heart was pounding in his chest like a hammer on an anvil as he gasped to fill his tightening lungs.

Mossa and Brook were well ahead of the soldiers, who had hesitated before following into the cornfield. Mossa was at the boat when Brook approached the swim. But Brook immediately saw Mossa freeze. Not a good sign, thought Brook. Then Mossa stood up slowly, a cocked gun to the back of his head and a Spaniard holding it behind him.

'*No te mueves*, or I kill him!' said the soldier with his eyes darting between Mossa and Brook.

Mossa looked wide-eyed at his captain and mentor, who had that resolute glazed glare, and he did not break in his brisk stride. He only looked back once to evaluate the advance of the soldiers approaching through the cornfield. Then he turned to the boat, in front of which Mossa was being held at gunpoint.

Brook only had one shot, one chance to make a getaway. With no time for second thoughts, he continued, carried as he was by his resolute momentum. 'I won't let them take you, Mossa. Open your mouth!'

Brook was too quick, too determined, and the black pirate did as he was told, not knowing what to think. In another two steps, Brook was a yard from the Spaniard and his prisoner.

'Sino le mato!' cried the Spaniard, who should have already carried out his threat by now.

It was too late because Brook had already poised his

pistol; he then thrust its barrel into Mossa's mouth. It was the only way: he had to kill the Spaniard standing behind Mossa as quickly as possible if he was to make a clean escape. Mossa's yelp of terror ceased the moment Brook pulled the trigger, and both Spaniard and captive fell simultaneously to the ground, each with a hole through his head.

Without glancing back, Brook threw his weight behind the rowboat, jumped in, and quickly put thirty yards between him and the arriving soldiers.

'Bollocks!' he yelled out as the soldiers brought their muskets to their shoulders. But it was not the ensuing volley that had made him cry out the expletive. It was the water at his feet, as he realised the Spaniard must have split the planks at the bottom of the boat to prevent any escape, and now it was taking in water fast.

ELEVEN

MAY HAD BEEN in some pickles in her long and varied life, but this took the biscuit. She was cold and wet, and she needed to pee.

'I need a moment alone, if you don't mind,' she said frostily to Ducamp, who had begun to walk in her steps.

'Oh,' he said, with an awkward rictus which he quickly shook off, and then said: 'Don't go far, mind! Meantime, I'll find some dry wood . . . Joe'll soon be back with a turtle. . .'

Two minutes later, May was squatting behind a skimpy tree amid a tuft of high grass. Inwardly, she cursed the impracticality of breeches, which she had to pull down to her knees. As she swiped at another mosquito buzzing around her nose, it suddenly occurred to her that she had left her trunk inside the boat at the clearing where the bosun was supposed to build a fire. To think, all he had to do was to push off into the water, and not only would she be stranded, she would have lost everything she had stolen from the *Bella Fortuna* as well as everything she owned. She cursed the impracticality of trousers again as she pulled them up and fastened the buckle.

But as she did so, she heard two male voices. The second

was as deep as Ducamp's, so it did not belong to Joe. Slowly, crouching from bush to bush, she advanced toward the clearing, where they had pulled the boat ashore so they could feed and camp for the night. The second gravelly voice she now saw belonged to Captain Brook, who had pulled a pistol on Ducamp, its barrel pressed to his temple. How the hideous captain had got there, she cared not: all she knew was that there was no reason why he shouldn't kill Ducamp and slip off in the boat.

She slunk as quietly as a bobcat into the clearing, now golden in the early evening sunshine. A moment later, she was aiming her cocked pistol at the captain's pockmarked face.

'Put it down, or I'll blow your ugly face off!' she said, not without dignity. But then, as soon as the captain gave a grunt of annoyance, Joe burst into the clearing all agasp, a turtle dangling from his shoulder.

'Joe, me lad!' exclaimed the captain, and in his jubilation, he lowered his pistol.

'Captain?' said Joe in surprise.

'What's wrong, Joe?' said May, taking command.

'We have to move out quick,' returned the lad, panic-stricken. 'There's Indians after me for taking their—'

All of a sudden, there came a volley of arrows, and before any of them could muster their thoughts, they were all dropping like coconuts onto the soft forest litter.

*

Tikama had made the journey from the valley of invincible beauty where the white tail deer drinks from spring-fed rivers to talk with the white chief of Saint Augustine.

He wanted his people to be more fairly treated he had

received reports of some of them having been worked to death to build the great walled fortress that even the fire-spitting ships could not destroy.

He had left with a close clique of attendees and warriors and at present had set up camp to the north of the township so they could observe the goings-on from a safe distance. He wanted to verify and understand the complaints of cruelty. If they proved to be true then he would retract from their agreement and take his people back to the lands where they were born and raised at one with nature where the healing forests surrounded their villages.

And he would have no qualms in doing so if the white man's written word was no better than when it was spoken out loud.

Some of his entourage were preparing their shell-tipped arrows dipped in poison for the hunt. They either killed the prey outright or put it to sleep so it could be eaten fresh later, just as the spider bites its prey and leaves it in a cocoon. He knew he was on a tough mission but he knew too that he had the hide of an old bison and he was not afraid of talking his mind. Had the gods not given him life thus far to watch over his people?

He was sitting smoking the tobacco that kept the mosquitoes at bay and appeased the worries of the spirit, when one of his men came running and bowing up to him.

'We have spotted a black man, a half-blood, my chief. He has taken the great turtle from the land of our fathers. What should we do?'

Tikama took another peaceful draught from his pipe. The mention of the ancient village whose ruins were now barely visible, engulfed as they were by nature's tendrils, took him back to when, as a boy in the summer he would taunt the great alligator with his arrows and whip up the black snake by the tail. Those were the days when the Spanish township was but a cluster of wooden huts, and his people outnumbered them by many scores. What had happened, he wondered, to set the gods against them, send them illness and disease and wipe out the great numbers of tribes that once filled the plains with the laughter of children and the song of old women.

And as if the white man was not enough, now the gods had sent the black man who was becoming more and more numerous, albeit in slavery. But Tikama sensed deep down that one day their numbers would replace the Timucua tribes completely if they were not culled. For they were strong, endowed with resistance to nature's curses and able to work under the crushing weight of the high sun.

'Follow him, take him,' said the chief. 'He must be a runaway slave sent to provide us if not with bargaining power then a gift to soften the brow of the white chief.'

The young warrior made a sign to his brethren and sped off soundlessly through the mangrove forest of their ancestors.

The chief took up his pipe again and tried to focus his mind on tomorrow's discussion with the white chief whom he nonetheless held in high esteem. For Tikama was sure that he would listen to his concerns over the treatment of his people, for he oversaw his own folk with just as much benevolence. But what to do with the black man? he wondered as he sipped the black drink from his shell cup.

*

Night was falling by the time May awoke.

It took a moment for her to understand where she was before realising that she and her companions had been captured. They had been transported to a dry area of the mangrove forest where a small fire blazed under the red-and-purple sky. She figured she must have been out cold for hours.

It soon became clear to her from the rudimentary camp that their Indian captors were living rough in these woods. Maybe they were on a hunting expedition. Or maybe they had been sent to track Captain Brook who was obviously on the run, otherwise why else would he be alone? Or maybe they were simply escaping the white man's harsh demands of labour, imposed on their people to build the fort at Saint Augustine.

Her thoughts were interrupted by the smell of grilled meat coming from another clearing. She could make out the glow of embers and the silhouette of a wooden *barbacoa* frame through the trees. Ducamp, lying next to her, gave a thick grunt as both he and the captain peeled open their eyes.

'Where's Joe?' said Brook, raised on one elbow and squinting up at the native guards before turning back to Ducamp. Didier gave a shrug while two Indian attendees came and offered them each a bowl of hot broth. The three captives were hungry and nodded their acceptance.

'Sure we can eat this?' murmured May, sniffing at the savoury dish that smelt distinctly coppery. 'It might put us to sleep again.'

'If you don't wannit, hand it over 'ere, Ladyship,' said Brook, which May did accordingly. 'Ha, if they wanted to kill us, they'd 'a' done it already! And as it ain't so they'll not be wanting to lug us around, will they!' He downed the broth, scooping the nuts and meaty chunks with his fingers. A few moments later, in a deep whisper he said: 'They've taken our arms. But I've still got a blade left in me pants. You?'

'In my leg,' said Ducamp.

'A gun up my sleeve,' said May.

Brook said: 'I reckon they're Timucua, and my guess is they're gonna wanna sell us to the Spaniards, so on first chance, we make a run for it. You with me?'

'They could also be on the run, couldn't they?'

'I wouldn't give a man who's just shot me with a poison arrow the benefit of the doubt, Ladyship, would you? Now, you with me?' Ducamp gave a hardly perceptible nod of the head. May nodded too. Then Brook said: 'But first, we find out where they've taken Joe.'

'Unless he got away,' said May. 'He knows his way round here.'

'Let's hope he comes back for us, then,' said Ducamp while Brook finished the bowl, which he followed up with a deep burp of satisfaction.

A little while later, the hawk-nosed chief, distinguishable by his furrowed face and torso, both heavily tattooed, came along with his entourage of young athletic men with bobbed hair whose only covering was a deerskin breechcloth and the tattoos they wore. 'We stay here this night, then we travel by boat in the morning,' he said in accented English.

'My men will come a'looking, chief. There'll be big trouble for you if you don't let us go now,' said Brook, in an attempt to take the upper hand.

But the old chieftain stood stoic, and he looked the three of them over as if evaluating their commercial value. Indeed, the Spanish chief would give the Indians a fine welcome with such a catch. For before sundown Tikama had received word of the attack on the Spanish township from a horde of thieves.

'Where's my mulatto?' continued Brook, impervious to

the chief's proud, steely gaze.

At length, in a slow voice of wisdom, the chief said: 'You steal our boat. Your boy steal our turtle.' Here Tikama flicked an eyelid at an attendant who threw a hand into Brook's lap. 'Your boy is now part of us . . . and you.'

Ducamp could sense the calm that preceded the storm as Brook processed the news of being fed his mulatto, Joe. Joe, the only human being he truly cared for. Joe, who he gave his bed to; Joe, who had gently cared for his wounds; Joe, who he had likewise taken care of. Dead and eaten.

May's hand flew to her mouth as the appalling notion of Joe's horrible fate sank in. She, too, sensed Brook's slowly rising surge of wrath, and she moved her hand from her mouth toward her pistol.

Brook covered his eyes as he looked down at the lad's gentle, slender hand, now paled, the only hand that had given him relief, the hand he had planned to pass on his treasure to when he died.

He then looked up, and from deep within his gut came a beastly, visceral cry, and then he roared: 'Bastards! You bastards! You BAST-AAARDS!'

The guards started at the terrible noise, then stepped forward to arrest the white captain as he quickly got to his feet. But it was too late: Brook was already brandishing a knife. Didier and May, riding with the action were quick to rally to Brook's side as he parried the first Indian's attack with one hand and jabbed him in the face with the other. He turned quickly to grab another Indian and, pulling back the man's head by his bob of hair on the top of his head, swiped his sharp blade deeply across the Indian's throat before swinging round to the next.

The chief was slipping away, taking with him three

attendees while giving the order for reinforcements to rally to their side. But his command was drowned out by a loud detonation coming from the woman who now stood with a smoking gun. Four Indians already lay on the ground, dead or wounded.

Ducamp read the captain's next move and swiftly strode toward the attendees, who were backing off with their chief behind them.

Brook was in an invincible mood. Blood was seeping from a shoulder slash, but he did not feel a thing. He only had one objective in his sights, and he lunged straight for the chief, ignoring the attendees.

There was another loud shot that rent the humid air, making birds flutter and scatter from the long grasses and mangrove trees all around. Ducamp seized his chance to get to the chief before Brook, who only had one thing in mind, and that thing would not serve their purpose of escape. For Ducamp knew that Brook's intense glare meant there would be no negotiation if the captain reached the chieftain first.

Didier quickly wrapped a strong, thick arm around the chief's neck, and pushed the point of his knife against the craggy throat so it made an indentation; any further, and the pressure would draw blood. 'Get back!' he shouted. He then flicked his eyes at Brook, who registered Ducamp's objective. Brook gave a nod in return, having figured, too, that the river must be behind them, judging by the deep bellows and purrs of gators.

'The boat!' growled Brook at the chief as Ducamp held him. 'Where's the boat!' he repeated, shouting his demand while Ducamp again pressed the knife hard into the chief's throat, to the limit before letting blood.

The proud chief said nothing. Tikama was ready to die

here on the ancestral land where he used to come as a boy in the summer. It was a fitting place to join the spirits of the ancients, he thought. But the attendees pointed in front of them, which confirmed Ducamp's assumption that the river must be behind him.

At the same time, May directed her pistol at the attendees who stayed rooted to the spot. It was a bluff, for she had already unloaded it.

The three of them edged back into the dark vegetation, Ducamp pulling the chief with him. The attendees followed, keeping their distance.

'No good, bosun,' said Brook. They want him back, and they won't let us go until they have him. Give 'im to me,' he ordered.

'No, you'll bloody kill him, and we'll be dead meat,' growled Ducamp.

'I'll 'old 'im while you make for the river!' said Brook, grasping and pulling the chief's wrist with force so that Ducamp had no choice but to pull away his blade or risk slicing his captive. The captain soon had the chief tightly within his grasp, his knife firmly on his throat. He gave a dastardly grin as he nodded to Ducamp. 'I'll hold him till I count to thirty, no more. Now piss off!'

The look in the man's eye told Didier he was determined to get his way, come what may.

'Let's go!' said May, with a quick tug at the bosun's wrist. Together, they crept back, creating more distance between Brook and his captive. Ducamp knew the Indians would have their sights uniquely on their chief, for the moment. He also knew that Brook's countdown was often shortened. It was one of his favourite tricks. He used to say it was to put the prey out of their misery quicker.

As soon as they had put ten yards between them, Ducamp turned. May had done the same, and simultaneously, they put on a sprint through the gloomy mangrove undergrowth, once each tripping on the protruding roots of trees.

'No, this way,' said May at a natural fork in the path that reflected the ruddy hue of the evening sky. Being closest to the river, she could hear the deep, throaty growl of a gator. Ten yards later, they could see the dark, shimmering waters of the brackish river through the undergrowth. Then May saw the tree where she had squatted. It was not difficult to tell, for she now saw that she had left her waist sash behind. No time to retrieve it now, for behind them, there came a great, mad roar and the loud, whooping cries of Indians.

Timucua's spirit soared with the eagles to the afterlife where the great chiefs of the Timucua had travelled before him. His people would not be defended tomorrow after all. They would not be led back to their homeland. Instead they would die in servitude.

Ducamp sensed Brook must have got his revenge; now he would fight the attendees until he went down. There came more booming roars through the forest, then nothing, while back at the clearing by the river, May and Didier were confronted with an unexpected welcome party.

'Woah!' cried out Ducamp, clenching May's arm before she ran into the path of an eleven-foot alligator. The great beast lunged forward, clapping its huge snout open and shut. Ducamp quickly realised it was coveting the dead turtle that still lay where Joe had left it.

'This way,' said May, who threaded her way back through the dark undergrowth to the other side of the rose-coloured clearing. The boat was still there, and the trunk too. They pushed the boat into the water while the sound of pounding feet through the undergrowth came closer.

'Wait!' called Ducamp, detecting that only one person was making them.

It was a gasping Brook who suddenly appeared on the far side of the clearing while other feet came rumbling behind. His blade was dripping with blood, his tunic sopping, and the stump of a broken arrow was planted in his upper arm as he stood, panting heavily for a moment to take stock, placing his hands on his knees.

'Nooo!' cried out May. The captain detected a movement in the corner of his eye, but his aching legs were now lacking in reflex, and his thoughts were sluggish.

'Shi-iiit!' he cried out as the alligator lunged up and clapped its jaws around the captain's arm. The massive creature tugged at the man, bringing him down, and dragging him inexorably to the water's edge. Ducamp jumped out of the boat, while amid the cries of the victim, there came the sound of furious whooping from the forest. And suddenly, the Indians were at the clearing. Ducamp jumped back to the boat as the alligator flipped itself into a roll and edged back into the water, taking with it the captain's arm, torn from the shoulder.

There was nothing Ducamp could do. He pushed the boat off into the current while May took up the oars, the captain now on his feet and swiping wildly with his remaining arm that had not let go of his knife. Didier jumped into the boat and grabbed the other set of oars. May and Ducamp pulled hard with the river tide, which at that time of day was pushing the slow waters northward.

Ten yards out, and the cries of the captain were no more as May gave another stroke and saw the Indians tying Brook's ankles.

'They'll either eat him to pass on his courage into their own bodies,' said Ducamp, 'or leave him for the gators.'

'Well, you gotta admit, he was a bloody nasty bastard,' said May. 'What now?'

'Just keep rowing!' returned Ducamp as an arrow skimmed the side of the boat.

TWELVE

A WOMAN ALONE with her trunk in a mangrove forest was bad enough, thought May. A woman alone with a pirate was sheer madness.

What stopped him from having his way with her then, taking off with all her worldly possessions? Nothing. She sensed there was still something left of his moral fibre. However, now that she had made him her protector, what would he expect in return? Did he want treasure? Most pirates did—treasure to buy their way through life, to buy food, drink, women, and a wife to give them children. But there was one thing they could not buy: the love of a woman, thought May.

'Best put in there,' said Ducamp, interrupting her thoughts and pointing to the right bank. 'Before it gets too dark.'

'Doesn't look like such a good spot to me,' said May. 'What if we get attacked and eaten?'

'Won't matter long as you're dead, will it!'

'There is an array of things that can happen between being caught and eaten, Monsieur Ducamp. And I do not want to experience any of them. Let's keep going.'

'It'll soon be pitch-black.'

'We can navigate by starlight,' returned May. Ducamp looked dubiously at the sky that was quickly losing its red tinge. May persisted: 'The sky will be clear of clouds.'

'If we don't put in now,' said Ducamp, 'it'll be too late to see where we're putting our feet, let alone our backsides, if you'll pardon the expression.' So Ducamp directed the boat to the water's edge. He then jumped into the shallow water and proceeded in dragging it onto the shore. It was the sensible thing to do.

'As long as the tide doesn't come up too high,' said May.

'It'll be fine if we pull it up high enough . . .' said Ducamp. But as he said this, May's face suddenly froze in horror. Ducamp quickly turned to face the object of her shock and saw the terrifying jaws of a female alligator. Then he saw the butt-end of an oar as it jabbed the massive creature in the muzzle, so deflecting its course just enough. Ducamp thrust the boat forward and sprang back inside it in the space of seconds.

'You were saying, Monsieur Ducamp?' said May. Ducamp's only answer was to clasp the oars with his large hands and heave away. Now laughing out loud, May continued: 'I've never seen a man hop so fast!'

Ten minutes later, they came to a fork in the creek. 'To the right will take us nearer the coast,' said May. 'There, at least, we won't be competing with alligators; they don't go in the sea,' she said with a teasing laugh. Without a word, Ducamp paddled to the right. They put into the shore along a spit of sandy land, on the other side of which could be heard the breaking ocean waves.

*

'Now what?' said May an hour later as they sat around the small fire. They had heaved the boat the short distance to the ocean-facing beach, and had built a camp behind it.

Ducamp brought his flask of grog from his lips and passed it to May, which she took to moisten her mouth. He said: 'There's another Spanish mission further in land, Tolomato. Either we head out to sea without a sail, and pray to God the currents take us to Charles Town, or we steal a sail from the mission.'

May passed him back the flask as she said: 'Or we could just buy one.'

'Buy one?' replied Ducamp as if it were an absurdity. 'We'll be as good as selling ourselves to the enemy.'

'Don't see why. The Spanish are supposed to be on the same side as the English, remember?'

'And the French?'

'You can be my indentured man.'

'And why would I be leaving France to be enslaved to an English lady?'

'Because the English lady's husband died of distemper?'

'Don't rhyme; I would never have left to become someone's slave,' said Ducamp, looking out to sea.

'So why did you leave France then?' returned May in a softer tone of voice.

'Told you before, in the name of freedom,' he said, gazing back into the fire.

'Did you leave anyone behind?'

After two beats, he looked across at her and said: 'Bones in a grave. And you?'

'I only look to the future. America is my home now.'

'Family?'

'My husband is dead. I told you. And you?'

'Same. Wife and child.' The notion suddenly filled him with grief as the embers of the fire warmed his face. He stood up, took a step seaward, and cast his eyes over the dark horizon.

'What is it?' said May, keeping her eyes from prying into his sudden emotion. Instead, she got to her feet and joined him in looking out to sea.

'A Dutch merchantman. Coming to anchor,' he said. She placed her hand on his bare forearm. He did not flinch from the touch but continued: 'When they died, they took everything I had inside.'

'I know,' said May softly. 'I know.'

After a couple of beats Didier continued in a more dispassionate tone. 'I speculate she'll be waiting to come ashore further up, with the morning tide.'

'What are we waiting for then!' exclaimed May.

'Like this?' returned Ducamp, his voice brighter.

'You are my indentured servant, remember? We managed to put ashore before our ship was taken by pirates.'

'Not plausible.'

'It happens more than you think. Aren't we the living proof?'

'No, I say. And I'm not being anyone's servant!'

'Not even for half the treasure in that trunk?'

*

After breaching the surf, they managed to pull the boat alongside the merchantman. While May held the rowboat against the ship, Ducamp proceeded to climb the side of the vessel, in order to notify the captain. A short while later, May boarded, and the gig was put on tow.

'Thank you, Didier,' she said, quite under control. Turning

back to the captain, a well-mannered Dutch merchant, she said: 'Captain, we have escaped our ship taken by pirates.'

'Your manservant told me in so many words, Madam.'

'Please know that I can pay our passage. Where are you headed, if I may ask?'

'Charles Town,' he said. May laughed with joy inside, which had the effect of smoothing over the pleat of concern on her brow. However, the captain put up a hand as if to ward away any high expectations and said: 'But before that, we're stopping at San Mateo. The Spanish mission always has a fair stock of wheat to trade, and we need to water before we head up the coast.'

'Oh,' said May, concealing her disappointment with a straight smile. 'Then we shall bide our time with gratitude.'

'You'll have to take the lower deck, I'm afraid,' continued the captain. May knew what that meant; it meant having to use the bucket, but she tried her best not to look exasperated. He then headed back to his cabin, leaving May to wonder why the man did not pay her more attention. Did she look so awful? she wondered. Surely not in the lamplight, though, not to mention she had tried to fix herself up before leaving the beach. Or were her looks suddenly betraying her?

After he had helped a mate lug the trunk below deck, Ducamp turned to May and said: 'One o' the lads told me the captain's got a dalliance in San Mateo; apparently, it's his last port of call before joining his family in Charles Town.'

'I'd be surprised if he did any dallying now. But that would explain it, though,' said May, relieved to know that the captain had no doubt been planning on satisfying his husband's itch.

'Explains what?'

'Oh, nothing . . .'

'You mean why he didn't treat you like a fine lady?' said Didier. 'I'd be thankful he let us board at all.' Then he turned in for the night on a hessian sack filled with straw, leaving May to wonder if she really was losing her charm.

*

Early next morning, the merchantman entered the wide estuary that only two nights earlier, Ducamp had travelled up with Brook and his men. And now Joe and Brook were dead and probably both eaten. Most of the crew must also be dead or soon to hang, thought Ducamp, and he wondered about the *Bella Fortuna*. Maybe she had been wrecked during the storm while the men were sleeping. Ducamp had no remorse; their passage on this earth would not be missed by anyone. He was glad to have escaped the hellish ship, and thinking about, it was all thanks to her.

He remained aboard while she took up the offer to make landfall. It would have seemed suspicious if the lady did not take the opportunity to refresh her person ashore. While Ducamp pondered the destruction of the lives that the pirate raid had caused, May sat as dignified as she could, now clad in her pilgrim's attire in the rowboat that took her, the captain, and a number of mates up the San Juan River to the gently sloping shore of the mission settlement.

It was a morose place if ever there was, she thought to herself, after disembarking. The cortege ambled under a dull sky, up the mudded track between the indenture dwellings and outhouses to the palisade gate where they were met by the commander.

'My friend, I fear you come at a tragic time. We have suffered a raid by pirates who have left two good men dead and our stores depleted. We are in desperate need of provisions.'

'I am very sorry to hear that, Commander. I take it that you have nothing to trade then?'

'Alas, they have even taken our grain. All we have left is our livestock and whatever is standing in the fields.'

'So sorry to hear that. I do empathise, Commander,' said May, joining the conversation in Spanish. 'I only wish there were something I could do.'

'Ah, allow me to introduce Señora Stuart,' said the captain to the Spanish commander. We picked her and her indenture man up after they escaped from their ship taken by pirates.'

'Indeed, Señora,' returned the Spaniard, turning to the lady with a slight bow of condescension. Nevertheless, May instinctively detected the commander was not insensitive to her sovereign beauty and refined posture. 'Could it be the same that raided our stronghold? What did they look like?'

May did not want to give too much away, given that she was harbouring one of them. 'I believe they were led by a certain Captain Brook, Commander,' she said, as they made their way across the compound. 'Alas, that is all I can say.'

'How did you escape?'

'At night, while they went ashore. We were able to steal away in the gig.'

'Incredible,' said the commander. 'But I should like to speak with your manservant, if I may, Madam. He may have valuable information on the villains. We cannot bring back the dead, nor can we recover the fruit of our labours, but if we could hang the wretches, then I for one would be able to look the widow in the eye.' He nodded toward the little wooden chapel, and then added: 'And tell her that her husband's callous killer has gone to hell!'

A little while later, May found herself paying her respects in the chapel before the two bodies. A widow was kneeling in front of one of them with two young children on either side of her, looking forlorn. May gave her condolences, and, brushing aside the emotive nature of the situation, in Spanish, she said: 'I shall send you something to alleviate your suffering, Señora.' The young woman—who May sensed was in a desperate state of mind, not just because she had lost her husband, but also because of her uncertain future—brushed away her tears, swallowed a sob, and gave thanks.

Life had taught May to be practically minded in this way, to move on quickly for the sake of self-preservation. It had typically been her own line of conduct in times of difficulty over the years: to move on, think of the future, and try not to let grief take a hold. It was what the midwife had told her when she miscarried the first time she fell pregnant to a forger, all those years ago in England. It turned out to be a blessing in disguise. First, the forger was caught and executed with his gang before she was three months pregnant. Second, she did not want to risk dying in childbirth. But more than anything, she remembered the midwife's words—words which she now found herself echoing to the widow: 'You must think to the future now. You are still young and pretty. You must find a new husband.'

Visibly relieved, the widow nodded and gathered her children into her clutch. 'Si, Señora,' she said bravely, 'you are a saintly woman. Thank you kindly . . .'

'My manservant will bring back a hamper,' said May, with a fleeting glance to the governor. He responded with a nod of assent which May took to mean that he would take care to find her a new husband.

It had become May's habit to always think how she could get the best out of a situation, and here it was no different. Indeed, she had mentioned the hamper not only to bring relief, but also to put herself in a saintly light in the eyes of the woman, which the commander would not fail to acknowledge, making any suspicion of her person all the more awkward to follow up. It was part of a plan that might save Ducamp from being recognised and consequently executed. But first, she had to know what had really happened here. For was he not an accomplice to the cold-blooded murder of defenceless men? His life was in effect at present in her hands.

*

'I told Brook there should be no innocent victims. I told you,' said Didier in a low voice the following morning.

May had returned to the ship at daybreak with a jug of goat's milk, having spent the night in the mission settlement, where she had been able to bathe without the risk of being ogled by male folk. She had accepted to stay at the Spanish widow's dwelling, and had dined at the commander's table with the ship's captain. She had then spent part of the night thinking how she would get around the commander's repeated demand to speak with her manservant. Before leaving, she had reiterated her promise to the widow, who gave her the fresh milk for the voyage.

'Is that why they flogged you?' returned May to Ducamp in French and in whisper.

Ducamp gave a curt nod, then said: 'Look, I was about to intervene when Brook gave the countdown, but he shot the poor bastard on three. I swear to God!'

May needed to hear it again. She needed to hear the sincerity in Didier's hushed voice and see it in his eyes. A

172

few moments later, she returned with a leather tankard which she handed to him, saying: 'Drink this.'

'What is it?'

'Poison . . .'

'What?'

'It will kill you or save your life, but it's your only chance. If they recognise you, they will string you up on the nearest tree!' Ducamp said nothing as the seriousness of the situation hit home. May continued. 'If you trust me, take it.'

He looked into the lady's eyes, her beautiful, unblinking, bright eyes. Taking advantage of the moment, he let his gaze travel up to the pleat of concern upon her brow; up to her soft, scented hair, and down to her sensual mouth. If this was the last thing he would see in this world, then so be it, he told himself. There could not be a prettier picture . . . Then he took the leather tankard and downed the draught in one go, so that it hit the pit of his stomach even before the bitterness had time to leave a sour taste in his mouth.

May proceeded in preparing the hamper as promised. It was the least she could do, and it came with the added advantage of relieving her of some of her own guilt. For had she not passed on the intelligence of the payroll hoard to Ducamp, Brook would not have stupidly mistaken the mission settlement for Saint Augustine, and the woman's husband would not be lying in a wooden box now.

By the same token, if she had not passed on the intel to the French governor, young sailors' mothers would not soon be mourning their sons. But May did not dwell; there was no point. Those lads would have been sent to fight in the Caribbean; the widow's husband could have had an accident or come down with a fever . . . No, what counted now was that she was in a position to offer some kind of physical comfort, and that she embraced it with gratitude.

She included some clothing from her trunk, undergarments, which any woman would gladly use to secure a suitor's ultimate admiration, and three gold coins in a drawstring pouch, along with a note reiterating their discussion of the previous day. She also included her favourite robe—the robe she had unable to cast out the ship window—which the woman could sell or use if need be. Anything was better than being destitute, May thought to herself, and didn't she know it.

Two hours after Ducamp had taken the poison, the hamper was passed down into the longboat. It had been sent by the captain to transport barrels of wheat, which a party of mates and two villagers were to row back up the San Juan River. May asked both of these men to follow her down into the damp middeck, where Ducamp lay in a corner on his straw-filled hessian sack in a cold sweat. The skin around his sunken eyes had turned purple, his face was livid, and his skin clammy, like that of a man at death's door. In short, what May showed the villagers was a pale reflection of what her servant had been that very morning, unrecognisable even. He looked like a man in the throes of a terrible distemper, so much so that the Spaniards took two paces back. May shook his shoulder and said softly but with authority: 'Didier, these men have come to take you to the mission which those pirates sacked.' Ducamp lifted his head and looked feebly around, the whites of his eyes streaked with veins, his pupils black pinpricks. 'Do you remember anything about them? Their names?'

'Brook, a captain Brook, and a . . . Mattis . . .' said Ducamp, with a gulp every couple of syllables in an attempt to secrete saliva to lubricate his dry throat. He then let his heavy head fall back on the hessian sack.

May turned to the villagers and said: 'I fear he may not be able to travel ashore . . .'

'No, no,' said one of them, 'he must stay here. We've already had our share of misery without bringing the distemper within our midst.'

'Then please tell the governor the names, and that I regret to find my servant in no fit state to go ashore . . .' The Spaniards nodded vigorously, one of them crossing himself, and lost no time making their way out into the sea air and back to the boat, no doubt fearing a contagion.

It took all of May's persuasive powers to convince the captain to isolate Ducamp on the orlop deck, where she affirmed she could save him with her medicine chest. She assured him that the sickness was not contagious, just a passing distemper. Moreover, the villagers would not allow him to enter their village anyway, whether she had generously left a hamper for the widow or not. So, once the captain had completed his business, they sailed on to Charles Town with a delirious Ducamp, his liver fighting to recover from the arsenic that May, in her zeal to save him from certain death, had overdosed more than she had intended.

The ensuing night and day, May rarely left his side. She made him drink tankards of milk, and repeatedly, she sponged down his body to lower the temperature, as though she were a goddess sculpting a new man; a well-made man at that.

During his delirium, he spoke of his past, of his aspirations, of his disillusions and loss of his family. In return, May recounted in a whisper her life in England, her life as a "consort," before she was able to concede what she really had been: a spy and a high-class courtesan. Too weak to counter her story, Didier simply listened, and accepted. 'I have no regrets, and yet I am not proud, but at least I have enough treasure to never bow down to a man again,' she concluded defiantly. But even in his semi-delirious state, Ducamp understood that her defiance was more a device to fathom his thoughts than a stance of rebellion against him.

He murmured: 'Let he who is without sin cast the first stone.' Didier had marked the saying in the Bible that his Huguenot friend had given him, not so much for any religious fervour as for the novelty of finding the original quote he had sometimes heard spoken. But when he said it now, it seemed to have a completely appropriate ring about it, something spiritual even. Could this woman, a fallen woman as he was a fallen man, really be an angel come to save his soul?

*

For May, the sight of the calm waters of the natural harbour and the new city walls of Charles Town was like a homecoming.

She enjoyed the clement air here, the surrounding farmsteads and their green fields that spread out from the ramparts. But she would not be stopping in the township with its perpendicular streets and new stone buildings that had grown in number since last she had put into port. Instead, she would be heading across town, straight through the city gate that led into the countryside dotted here and there with farms and fine fur merchant houses. Relations with the local tribes had always been good, and the fur trade had enabled the town to quickly prosper.

From the main deck, she noted the harbour seemed busier than before, with tall ships in the roadstead waiting their turn to slip into quay while the tide was high. Once ashore, she thought to herself, she knew what she would do.

She had no time for lingering in town to see the new developments, as pretty as they now were. She would head straight for the country in a French carriage and travel northward for a mile and two furlongs until she came to Mrs Moore's house. Mrs Moore was the gentle-mannered widow of a furrier and lived in a large house on a small plot of land. It was the house which her husband had built for her and their son—their son who, nowadays, was more often than not out trading with Indians for skins in the backcountry as far as the Chattahoochee River—and which she refused to leave.

May was impatient and nervous at not knowing what she would find there, so much so that she gave a slight start when a male voice spoke near her turned ear.

'So this is the end of the road, is it?' The voice belonged to Ducamp.

Quickly regaining her composure, May delicately picked a rebel strand of hair from her forehead and said: 'Not quite, Monsieur Ducamp. We have yet to get my trunk home.'

'You're expecting me to come with you as a servant?'

'Have you any other suggestion? You hardly have the appearance of anyone higher. Besides, it is part of our agreement. I pay you only on arrival.'

'All right, then,' returned Ducamp tetchily. 'I hope this treasure's worth it!'

'I certainly think so,' said May. 'I shall stand ready to disembark and hire the first horse and cart. Otherwise, we'll have to use a handcart.'

'I'm not going on a country hike in this heat,' said Ducamp, who, though he would not say it, was still feeling feeble after the bout of poisoning—poisoning that had nonetheless saved his life, so he couldn't grumble.

177

'And I'd rather not stay the night in town,' said May, keener than ever to reach Mrs Moore's house.

An hour later, Ducamp, May, and the trunk were being transported through the town gate and onto the road that led northward. It had been a scorching day, and the wind that blew through their hair came as a refreshing caress along the leafy earth track. Ten furlongs out, where the land was still laboured, a house nestled in a plot came into view. It was a stone building, set amid a few acres of farmland mostly given over to tobacco. Fretful and anxious, May wondered how she would be received. Would the girl remember her face even?

Once her foot hit the sun-baked earth, she gave a word to Ducamp and the driver about where to put the trunk. Then, raising her skirts, she dashed off to meet an old lady who had come out of the open door and was now standing on the porch, holding a child's hand.

Ducamp cast a dubious eye at the carter. 'I'm not her servant,' he said.

'Everyone's a servant to May,' said the old man with a chuckle. 'She has beauty!' Then he climbed down from his seat and said: 'Come on, let's do as she says. Then I can get a drink and a bite to eat and be off.' As they went to fetch the trunk, Ducamp kept an eye on the welcome scene going on at the front door. He had a nasty feeling as he watched her greeted with tears by the old woman, and saw May pick up the shy child, hug and kiss it like it belonged to her. Ducamp was soon to find out that it did.

'My treasure,' said May, a few moments later introducing a bright little girl of five.

Ducamp gave a frown instead of a smile as he and the carter put down the trunk in the shade of the porch.

'Look, I'm sorry,' said May a short while later. Ducamp was smoking in front of the west-facing façade; it was late in the day, and the birds had increased their song. 'If I had told you, you might not have come this far.'

'There's trust for you! But now you've found your treasure, what about mine? Or was that all a lie to help you get here too?'

'No, most of it's in there.' Ducamp glanced down at the trunk. 'I already told you, I took the liberty of relieving the captain of some of the plate he kept pointlessly in his cabin.'

Ducamp turned back as the cart man hollered goodbye. May gave a nod and waved him off. Then she turned back to Ducamp. 'You must stay here for the time being, Monsieur Ducamp,' she said as the horse trotted off down the track.

THIRTEEN

DIDIER DUCAMP AWOKE to light streaming through the cracks in the shutters.

It felt good to wake up in fresh linen sheets in a soft feather bed. He could detect the aroma of coffee, an aroma he had come to appreciate more than the bitter taste of the beverage itself, which he nonetheless enjoyed when sugar was added. He looked around the whitewashed room, neatly and simply furnished: a bed, a table, a chair, and a *kasten*, which was a carved wooden cabinet where he imagined linen was kept. Then his eyes fell upon the tattered clothes lying on the floorboards and remembered how he had peeled them off like a second skin, for he had not changed them since leaving Nassau with Brook two months earlier.

There came a knock at the door. May, impeccably dressed, her hair soft and silky and smelling of roses, stood in the doorway.

'I've got some clothes for you,' she said with a hint of irony in her voice, 'so you can move up in rank from indentured servant.' She took a step into the room and left the folded pile on the chair. 'And some boots,' she said, waving to her daughter, who was holding one boot in each hand on the threshold. The child promptly dumped her load on the floor. 'Daddy Boots,' she said, then gave a cheeky chuckle and went back to clutch her mother's dress. Ducamp, lost for words, simply gave a nod. May left the room.

What did she want of him? he wondered. And apart from his share of treasure, what did he want of her?

The cart driver had told him that the English ship in port was headed north. So he had the choice to head back to Jamaica, where the wandering souls of the world found a sanctuary, or head north. He enjoyed the colours, the sunshine, the drink, and free living of Port Royale, and it was where he had come across Jacob Delpech as they sailed out of port. He was the Huguenot who had given Didier his Bible, which he had kept, for some reason not wanting to part with it.

The next instant, another knock on the door preceded the black middle-aged maid, who stepped across the room with a steaming jug. She poured water from it into the tub that Didier now perceived by the window.

*

May was sitting in a rocking chair on the front porch, taking in the gentle air of the country.

She wondered how much longer she could open doors with a smile. The experience with Brook, who cared not a bit if she smiled or cried at him, was edifying. Of course, he had no love of women, but it was still perhaps a taster of times to come. For regular gentlemen did not look at old women either. At least, not in a way that would enable her to open those doors. She would have to lead through personality, she thought to herself, not so easy in a man's world. There again, she still had plenty of door-opening days before her yet.

At peace with the world now that she had means, she watched her daughter water some flowers with a clay watering pot. She would need a father figure, thought May. Yes, all in all, May was getting used to the thought that she would still need a man. One who would love her in the morning, and when she was sick and ugly, and who would take her love at face value, not because she was a woman of means.

She knew what she required, and now she knew what she wanted, she thought to herself. Moreover, she had her needs.

May pushed herself up from her ponderings. Then she went inside the house, where she could hear the splash of water coming from inside the bedroom where Ducamp had slept. Why did he not make a move? Did he have feelings for her? She had to know. She had to know now.

She went to her room and prepared her medicinal accessories. She perfumed her hair, picked up her tray, and went to his room. Holding the tray in one hand, she knocked on the door. She entered without waiting for an answer.

Ducamp had just put on the clean clothes. She had chosen the most ample to make up for his being slightly bigger than her late husband. He stood before her in the blue linen breeches and white undershirt still unlaced at the chest, his damp hair pushed back, and then she knew. Deep down inside, she knew she could use this man, and she could make him good. Make him fulfil his promise.

'They fit,' he said, feeling slightly awkward. May noticed he said nothing of her barging in. Instead, he pushed back a rebellious strand of hair over his ears.

'They suit you,' she returned, thinking to herself how clean and rugged and strong he looked. 'Take a seat and remove your shirt.' She almost gasped at hearing her own words. 'I—I want to examine your wound. I—I don't want you leaving this place without having repaired my wrong.'

A frown momentarily darkened Didier's brow, but he did as she asked and sat down on the chair while May placed her tray on the table. 'Where will you go?' she said as she ran her fingers lightly over the stitches.

'Where every other lost soul goes in this New World. To Jamaica.'

'And spend all your money and then go out pirating again.'

'No, I'm not a pirate.'

'Privateering, pirating, same thing. Hold still.' She pressed the wound and made him wince.

Her soft hair brushed against his skin. He looked down at her as she pushed a long curl behind her ear to reveal her jawbone and her slender neck, and the intoxicating smell of roses filled his sinuses. He raised his hand slightly so that her hair brushed against it. The light touch made him melt inside. And he felt sexual desire rising. A desire mingled with roses and softness. Did she realise she was bewitching him? She was sharp; he liked that. She was sharper than he was, so she must know what she was doing, mustn't she? The last time someone offered their neck in such a defenceless way, he thought to himself, he sliced it through. But the horrible battle scenes quickly slipped from his thoughts as he became invaded by the touch and smell of May.

'It's not infected,' she said as she pulled up her head. 'So I can send you . . .' Then she noticed the pools of his eyes, that unmistakable look of a man suspended in love. She locked eyes with him as she continued: 'On . . . your . . . way . . .' With each syllable, they brought their faces closer. She instinctively placed her hands on his powerful torso. Then they abandoned themselves to the moment and fell into each other's embrace, their lips lightly touching. The sensation of mouths joining together, bodies coming close, removed any anxiety, and after the long kiss, he placed his large hands on her waist, then placed his half-open mouth onto her silky-soft neck. She drew slightly away under the tickly prickles of his beard, nudged his cheek, and searched blindly for his soft lips again as she let him sweep her up and carry her to the bedstead, both suspended in desire.

She pushed him aside so her knowing hands could more freely explore his body; then she undid her blouse and deftly slipped it off until she was in nothing but her shift. He let her take command, her knowing touch bringing him almost to a climax before she placed her hands on his bare chest so she could easily straddle him.

A while later, the clopping of horse hoofs outside the window clicked at the back of her mind. She ignored it, gave herself entirely to the moment, and then lowered her body while he was still throbbing inside her, her bare breasts coming to rest on his muscular diaphragm, her lips coming to caress the curve of his deep chest . . .

*

May knew men had a short attention span, especially when it came to women, unless a woman could hold them on a different level.

She had seen the bovine-eyed look before. Sometimes, it lasted no longer than the duration of an ejaculation before their minds were taken elsewhere. And in this New World, the primal driver in terms of desire was money. And money always gave the upper hand to the one who possessed it. It was the same in love. But May did not want a money-centric relationship.

Hurried footsteps in the corridor outside the room alerted her before there came a pressing knock. 'May, come quick!' said a woman's voice urgently.

'What is it, Mrs Moore?'

'John tells me you must make haste.'

Moments later, May had slipped on her shift and was standing at the door she had half opened. 'Tell me again, slowly,' she said.

'There is a warrant for your arrest. There's a man from Havana who's been talking nonsense about you. Saying you sold secrets to the French. And the French are now our enemy!'

'Thank you, Mrs Moore,' said May. 'I need a moment to think.'

'Don't linger, my dear. If there's anything against you, don't linger.'

May could usually see beyond the chaos and invariably found the best course of action to take in two blinks of an eye. But now she was in a whirl of emotion as she pressed the door into the frame. 'Come with me to Jamaica,' said Ducamp, in a low voice, the length of him naked and still in the liberation of lovemaking. 'There's a ship leaving this afternoon.' She did not want to go south. South was where she had left her old life. The life where she had detached body and soul. Now she wanted to live as one with her child.

'There is a ship going to New York, but you must hurry,' said Mrs Moore through the door, then left May and her new man to think things through.

A short while later, Ducamp, who had finished changing, said: 'Come with me; bring the girl. We'll get a stake outside Port Royale, set up a plantation . . .'

'The sun down south makes people crazy,' said May as she sat on the edge of the bed.

'Northward is English; a bit further north is French. I could be hanged for desertion if I got captured.'

'No, there's no point in taking needless risks,' she said. Ducamp thought she said it with distance, but then she continued: 'How will we get the trunk aboard?'

*

Ducamp felt like a different man, dressed in his clean set of clothes, and having scraped away the bristles from his cheeks with May's late husband's sharp razor.

He gazed at May, who he would hardly have recognised, dressed as she was in puritan attire: a thick woollen dress and shawl, a white pinafore, and a sky-blue bonnet.

He offered her his hand as she descended the porch steps, where the horse and cart were waiting. Turning to Mrs Moore, she said: 'I have left something in the kitchen drawer for you. I will write when I arrive, dear Mrs Moore.'

'Come, come, this is not the time for sad goodbyes,' returned the old lady, nonetheless damming her watery eyes with her forefingers. She embraced May firmly, then placed her old, dry hands around the child's cheeks. 'Take good care of the child, and yourself. Now, be gone before the soldiers come knocking,' she said, swallowing back her emotion. 'And when they do I'll tell them you've headed up the Ashley River, looking to buy furs.'

An hour later, the cart came to a halt at the wharf of the Cooper River that flowed at the rear of the town and offered two slips so that ships could unload and load directly to and from quay.

Ducamp lifted the girl to the ground, then called for a young carter amid the streams of people coming and going. Ducamp was strangely nostalgic at hearing some people speak French. May had explained that these people could only be Huguenots fleeing persecution in France. Indeed, they had already built their church, which gathered a large congregation on Sundays: planters coming from far around; such was their devotion. Ducamp remembered how once upon a time, in another life, he had been part of the force of troops that pressured them into converting to the Church of Rome. Many of them would not, though, and one of those was Jacob Delpech. What would Delpech do now? he thought to himself for an instant. He would stand up for righteousness; he would steer well away from the unrighteous path and pitfalls that many a man fell into on reaching foreign lands and warmer climes. But they had already made their plan: they would take the ship headed for the southern seas. Ducamp helped the young carter lump the baggage and the trunk onto the handcart.

'Are you ready, ladies?' said Ducamp to mother and daughter. 'We should make haste; the ship won't be beaten by the tide!' May was about to hand over her baggage, but stopped in mid-movement and lowered it to the ground. 'What's wrong?' murmured Ducamp, sensing something awry.

Bowing her head, she said: 'I can't. Not yet.' She flicked her eyes toward the slip where the southbound ship was moored. Ducamp spied a troop of soldiers marching into the harbour from the far side of the half-moon quay. The wharf was crowded with last-minute packers and passengers, and the troops were a hundred yards away. They would not have seen her, mingled as she was in the bustling crowd of merchants, hawkers, and relatives who were seeing either their cargo or the passengers off.

'But we must get aboard quickly. The ship won't wait for the next tide,' insisted Didier.

'You go on; get the trunk aboard. They are not looking for a lone man. We'll join you once the coast is clear.'

Ducamp gave a nod to May and stroked the child's cheek. She smiled back at him. 'Can I come?' she said.

'No, we have to wait, darling, until everything is sorted.' May and Didier gave each other a complicit nod. Did Ducamp detect sadness in her eyes? But there was no time to dwell. First thing was to get out of there. He was, after all, a former French lieutenant, and she was wanted by the law on a charge of espionage of which he knew she was guilty. He heaved the cart to help the carter get the momentum going, then waved his beaver hat back at May while she waited with her child amid her baggage. He had not insisted when she told him she would keep it with her.

Half an hour later, Ducamp was sitting on the trunk middeck in the ship bound south. Where the hell was she? he wondered. He began craning his neck. If she did not come soon, she would miss the ship. It suddenly occurred to him that since they had become lovers, he had been swamped by his emotions. He had not been thinking straight. But now, as he sat waiting, he set his mind straight and began to think the situation through. May was a calculating spy, was she not? She had a whole history of duping people. Could this be a ruse to get him out of the way so she could head north with all her treasure intact? They had said she was wanted, but what proof did he have of this? Could she have set it all up? Could she have seduced him to better manipulate him? Could she have taken the other ship that was also due to leave with the tide? She might have planned for another carter to take her treasure aboard.

He had imposed his idea of escape to southern skies, even though she had not been keen, for she had originally spoken of going north. Why did she so easily concede to his way of thinking? He had put it down to her being in love, but wasn't even that out of character?

'Make ready to bring in the plank!' called the quartermaster out on deck, and there was still no sign of May. There was only one way to find out whether he was being duped or not. He pulled the key from his chain, then frantically unlocked the trunk. He looked furtively around the deck at the other passengers settling in for the voyage to make sure there were no prying eyes. Then he slowly lifted the lid. He saw nothing but fabric, a beautiful dress; a souvenir of what May had been, no less! He took it like an emotional slap on the cheek as blood rushed to his head. He plunged his hand further in, expecting to touch rocks under the soft silk, rocks to weigh down the trunk. But to his surprise, his hand fell upon smooth, hard objects shaped like plate, then smaller objects shaped like jewels. He opened the lid further and pushed aside the clothing that concealed the treasure. On top of the dress, he saw a note. He pulled it into a beam of light, and closed and locked the trunk. He read:

'My dear Didier, if you come upon this note and I am not by your side, it will mean I have been prevented from joining you, or have been forced to head in another direction. This is your half of the treasure, my love. It will set you up wherever you should choose to lead your life. I sincerely hope you find a good woman who deserves you,

189

who loves you as I truly do.'

He stood up, brought his hand to his forehead. He turned to scour the surroundings through the gun port. He did not see her. Remembering her desire to head north, he picked out the English ship the next slip down at Smith's quay. He saw soldiers marching in block formation toward it. He then picked out two figures, a woman and a child. May was joining the English ship, hurriedly climbing the gang plank, furtively looking in his direction. He waved widely through the gun port to her, but she did not wave back. Perhaps she was focussed on the approaching soldiers. He swiftly strode up the steps, taking them two and three at a time.

'Sir,' he said moments later to the merchant captain. 'My apologies, but I must disembark.'

'Can't be doing that now, can we, Sir,' said the captain. 'We'll miss the tide; you'll just have to get off further down the coast. Sorry, but I'm late enough as it is.'

Didier now realised he had the treasure, but he had the wrong treasure.

Panicked now, it became quickly clear he had a choice to make between two treasures. A chest of silver and gems that would set him up for life, or a treasured family, something to fight for and to cherish. It was economic freedom—the desire of every privateer in the Caribbean—or the love of a woman, a woman who loved him enough to hand him his freedom in a trunk full of treasure. Whatever he must do, he must do it now, he realized. A woman like May would not suffer to be usurped by a chest of silver. But there again, there could be a woman like May in every port, couldn't there? And widows were not uncommon in this part of the world.

*

She had ordered a carter to take her baggage to the northbound ship.

And now, clutching her daughter's hand, she hurried onto the main deck as the stream of soldiers marched squarely through the crowd in the distance. They might not have anything to do with her. There again, they might have already been to Mrs Moore's and found her gone, she thought to herself, and good old Mrs Moore in her insistence was bound to inadvertently put them on her trail.

She glanced over the bulwark with a yearning of the heart toward the Dutch southbound ship, beginning to raise the gangplank. She told herself that it would have been senseless to embark on a voyage back to the very place she had been trying to get away from. Besides, she would not subject her daughter to growing up in a land of vice, when she could offer her a better life where perhaps passions were more restrained under a colder climate.

It would have been just as senseless to have tried to restrain Didier. She knew that to retain the love of a free spirit, she would have to first give him a free rein. So she had used the arrival of the soldiers to deliberately cut him loose, and to allow his choice to be made in total liberty. Wasn't that one of the fundamental pillars of this new society, to choose your faith and your life as you saw fit, and with the people whom you saw as worthy?

But now, seeing the soldiers approach, she began to regret sending him away.

The commander of the soldiers called to the ship's captain to let him know they were to board.

May grabbed hold of Lili-Anne, who sensed her mother's anguish. She then carried her daughter down to the dim lower deck, where forty other passengers were settling for the voyage to New York. She prepared her plan, and she reminded Lili-Anne not to talk, not to say her name, not even to the soldiers if they asked. Instead, May would pretend to poorly understand English; she would speak in French.

She heard the terrible clamour of boots on the wooden steps that led down to the lower deck. She tried to steel herself, for she knew that a charge of spying meant the gallows.

The commander of the troopers stood in his impeccable red frock coat on the lower step for an interminable moment, scanning the groups of people, while his eyes got used to the lack of daylight. Then his gaze fell upon a lone woman and a child standing next to a barrel on its end. Nodding to his two subordinates, he directed his steps toward her. May clenched her daughter by the hand. She longed to hold her tight, but she knew that any excessive anxiety would give her away.

'Madam,' said the commander in English, giving a slight bow as he approached. 'What is your name, please?'

'Pardon,' said May in French, trying to retain her composure while putting on a confused face.

'Your name, Madam. What are you called? *Votre nom, s'il vous plaît.*' May had not anticipated the possibility that he would speak to her in French, albeit with a poor accent. 'Madame?' he insisted with a straight smile that underlined his hooked nose.

May was about to answer with her chosen false name when another male voice took the word out of her mouth. 'Ducamp, Captain,' it said. 'Please forgive my wife. She has not yet mastered the English language.'

A wave of relief spread across May's face as she turned to

see her fake husband. The captain turned to the tall stranger with a strong French accent. 'This is your wife, Sir?'

'And my daughter.'

'A Frenchman aboard an English ship in times of war, isn't that an oddity?'

'On the contrary, we are fleeing France.'

'I saw him board the Dutch ship a while ago, Sir,' interrupted a lieutenant.

There was always someone watching, thought May to herself in quiet frustration, wondering how in this world Ducamp would get out of that.

'Yes, I was fetching something I had left aboard,' said Ducamp without a pause. 'The captain had kindly kept it for me,' he lied.

'And what might that be, Monsieur Ducamp?'

Didier reached into his inner pocket. He brought out a thick, leather-bound book.

'A Bible?' said the captain, taking the words from the suspect's mouth and the book from his hand. 'Printed in French,' he continued after browsing through the pages.

'Yes, Sir.'

'Then you are a Huguenot.'

Ducamp gave a short bow. The captain handed him back his Bible and said: 'Then carry on, Sir, I wish you fair wind.' Turning to his men, he said, 'Nothing here,' and led them out.

May held Didier's large hand. She wanted to squeeze it, to wrap her arms around his neck, but she would have to control herself for the time being. Didier brought the child between them; the gesture felt natural, right and reassuring. He craved to kiss the child's mother, but restrain himself he must. Instead, he let her lay her head upon his shoulder.

May felt better, like a new person. And for the first time in such a long time, she felt secure. But then a few moments later, she suddenly looked up into his eyes and urgently whispered: 'Didier, where's your chest?'

'Right here,' he said, chuckling softly, bringing his palm to his bosom, and caressed her cheek with the back of his index finger. 'Right here with my treasure!'

FOURTEEN

AS THE SHIP entered the bay of New York, Didier reflected on his chances. He had indeed held and lost a fortune, he thought to himself, but had he not found a treasure?

He watched May sleeping, with her child snuggled into her body. She looked serene, dressed as she was in her plain clothing. In truth, they were both impostors. But who wasn't? Who didn't change their lives? Wasn't that why he came to this New World in the first place? He thought to himself that he would have to make an honest woman of May Stuart.

She opened her eyes to the cold grey day filtering through the deck hatch and the gun ports. 'I hear gulls. Are we there?' she said, her voice thick with sleep.

'We are arriving at New York.' She smiled back at him, then sat up and tidied her hair. He said: 'Are you ready to start over again?'

'I am.'

'Are you willing to be my partner?'

The abruptness of the question and the intensity of his brow quickened her thoughts that were still thick with sleep. But she had not been without running over the eventuality in her mind during the voyage. So, answering on the volley, she said: 'I am. But do you think you will be able to settle down in one place?'

'I do now.'

'Then I think we can make a good team!' She reached for his hand. He wrapped an arm around her and covered her child.

*

Half an hour later, Ducamp was on deck, eyeing the distant trees on the islands to the left and right of the ship as it passed through the bay.

'A marvellous place,' said the man next to him in French.

'You are French, Sir?'

'And a Huguenot like yourself, Sir,' returned the man. 'I overheard your exchange with the English soldiers in Charles Town. They're a bit edgy at the moment, you know, what with news from Europe and the war with France. And to be honest, aren't we all? The French are not that far to the north; they would gladly take hold of this port if the opportunity arose, I can tell you. What is your trade?'

'I was a soldier, a lieutenant in the French army,' said Ducamp, determined now not to hide his past. It was perhaps the first step to being genuine, he thought to himself.

'Interesting. I am a merchant from La Rochelle, part of a settlement north of New York, you know. We're calling it New Rochelle.' Why couldn't they wipe the slate clean and call it something original? thought Ducamp, but he just nodded his head. 'Bringing back supplies from Charles Town,' pursued the merchant. 'Aye, things are a bit strained at the present time, but it's a marvellous place. And I am sure, being a military man as you are, that your skills will be of great help to a fledgling colony, Sir. For now, you are American, and as an American, I bid you welcome!'

Sometimes, thought Didier, you might be better off not speaking about your past, at least not if you wanted to remove yourself from it and start afresh.

'No more soldiering for you,' said a woman's voice from behind him. May, holding Lily-Anne by the hand, joined him and took his arm.

'No, I'm no longer a soldier, Sir, I am a settler, and I'll be looking to settle my little family here in this new town.'

'And God bless you, Sir!' said the merchant. 'God bless you all!'

Enjoy this book?
You can make a big difference

Honest reviews of my books help bring them to the attention of other readers. If you've enjoyed this prequel I would be very grateful if you could spend just five minutes leaving a short review on the book's Amazon page.

Thank you very much.

MERCHANTS OF VIRTUE

(Based on a true story)

Book One of
THE HUGUENOT CHRONICLES
Trilogy

Excerpt

20 August 1685

AN HOUR AFTER sunrise, two raps of the doorknocker made Jacob and Jeanne look up from their draught of chocolate.

Jeanne, holding her belly with one hand, pushed back her chair, then made her way from the panelled dining-room to the spacious vestibule. She began to climb the wide dark-wood staircase to the upper rooms where her children still lay sleeping.

Jacob had hurried to the window in the adjoining study that looked onto the street. He now peered between the wooden shutters that had been pulled ajar to screen the room from the day's heat. The maid, with fear in her eyes, had moved into the vestibule and now stood at the front door waiting for the signal.

'It is one of Robert's servants,' said Jacob with a sigh of relief. 'Open the door, Anette, and let him in.'

It was that time of day when a large number of chamber pots were emptied out of upper floor windows and, in his precipitation, the lackey had trodden on a turd. He was scraping his shoe on the wrought iron boot scraper when the massive green door opened. He stepped inside the entrance hall which led to the study, the rear corridor, and the staircase. Inside the door stood a wooden bench where people could remove their street footwear and garments, but the lackey remained standing.

'Speak up, my boy,' said Jacob from the study doorway.

'Monsieur, my master has sent me to tell you that soldiers are entering through Moustier gate. They are in great numbers, some on foot, some on horseback. Even greater numbers, some say thousands, are entering through the gate of Villebourbon.'

Despite her imminent labour, Jeanne, who had paused on the intermediate landing, hurried up the stairs. She was normally of a calm and rational disposition and not subject to panic, however these days it was every Huguenot mother's angst that her children would be taken away from her. She knew how easy it was for powerful men to amend and interpret the law as it suited them. When Madame Larieux's husband died, the authorities took the opportunity of her mourning to assign her three daughters to a convent, so that they could be brought up in the religion of the state according to a new law.

Jacob sent word to his own lackey to forewarn his mother and widowed sister who resided in the west part of town, a stone's throw away from the recently demolished temple. In this way, word spread from family to family, and in its wake marched de Boufflers' army, an army made up for the most part of Swiss and German mercenaries.

*

202

The bells of Saint Jacques chimed the hour. Today might be the day the Huguenot safe haven would become Catholic again, thought intendant de la Berchère. It gave him a real sense of virtue and piety to win over the heretics and rid the generality of heresy, for the sake of national unity, for once and for all.

Unfurling a scroll that lay on his desk, he turned his head to the Marquis de Boufflers who was standing at his side with the Bishop of Montauban.

The intendant said: 'In accordance with your instructions, my Lord Marquis, with Monseigneur Jean-Baptiste-Michel, we have drawn up a list of Protestant homes to be billeted, here.' His forefinger ran down a long list of names. 'Along with the number of troopers they are to accommodate.'

The Right Reverend Bishop Jean-Baptiste-Michel Colbert, a large-shouldered and pot-bellied man in his mid-forties, gave a little cough. And in his beautiful tenor voice, he said: 'The numbers have been carefully pondered, my Lord, in relation to the type of house and the, shall we say, potential resistance that is likely to be encountered.'

'Excellent, Your Grace,' said the Marquis, who proceeded in opening a leather pouch he was holding. While pulling out bundles of printed billets he continued: 'All you do now is write the name of the owner on a billet, the corresponding number of soldiers, and sign it.' The last wad of printed billets fell onto the desk. 'The simplest plans often make for the most effective results,' he said with a flourish of the wrist.

The billets were filled out, signed, then passed on to the commanding officers of small sections of troops. This took some time, and it was not until past lunchtime that many sections were informed of their quarters which they then had to locate.

*

After taking note of his billet, Lieutenant Didier Ducamp glanced at the sun from the northern double-vaulted arcade of the main square where he and his men – four Germans, two French, two Swiss – had settled after the march into town. He cast his eyes to his left toward a cobbled lane. 'Right, men, rue de la Serre is that way, I wager. We'll be needing a townsman to guide us, preferably a Catholic!' he said in his dry humour, as much to himself as to his men half of whom could barely understand him anyway.

In truth though, the lieutenant really did not care what religion his guide belonged to, so long as he led them to their destination. He knew from experience that every man was made of the same stuff inside, he had seen men of every religion slaughtered on the battlefield. They all spilled their guts the same when their belly was sliced. They all bled red blood, and shat through their arses in a like manner. Besides, he was beginning to dislike this dragonnade business. It had been amusing in Pau at first traipsing through bourgeois' homes but now it was becoming tedious. It was not what the army was made for. That said, duty was duty and in another three years he might even retire with enough money to get a tavern and a new wife.

There happened to be a crowd of onlookers on the corner. They had stopped to witness the scene of a Huguenot toff flapping around at his townhouse where soldiers were piling in through the large carriage door.

'You there,' called the lieutenant designating a bourgeois who looked like he was enjoying the show. Ducamp, who was over six feet tall, strode the few yards that separated them. He had to raise his voice above the ambient din of bawled commands, Germanic grunts, marching boots, the clank of steel and horses stamping and snorting. He said:

'Do you know rue de la Serre? I'm looking for a tall house with a large green door. Belongs to a certain Jacob Delpech.'

'I do indeed, sir,' said the bourgeois, proud to be of service. He took a few strides out of the way of the din and said: 'It so happens I live opposite. It is a spacious townhouse. Monsieur Delpech is of a long line of nobles of the robe, you know, except for his father who was a physician, I believe. I am sure you will find all the comforts you require there.'

Ducamp liked jurists' homes: they were well organised and most of them were well stocked. Things were picking up. He was looking forward to a decent night's kip in a good bed. And he wondered if his new host had any worthy maids, or daughters.

'If you would be so kind as to show us the way there, we shall find comfort all the sooner, shall we not?' said Ducamp as a quip, though the humour in his voice was hardly perceptible.

Over the next few hours, the clamour of four thousand men of war gradually spread out in small sections like Ducamp's from the epicentre of the town. Some lanes were made of dark grey pebbles shaped like pork kidneys that marchers cursed, others were hard earth thoroughfares made dusty in the high noon sun.

*

The sickening ruckus of hobnailed boots on cobbles grew louder in rue de la Serre, as the banging of iron knockers on doors proliferated. Inside the tall house with the green door, Jacob, Jeanne and their three children came to the last verse of a favourite psalm as the doorknocker rapped with authority.

The song always helped Jacob Delpech fight down a feeling of panic in times of uncertainty. And he must remain in charge of his emotions. He was, after all, responsible for the safety and wellbeing of his family and household. And he could not deny they were all probably about to suffer, unless he put his faith to one side.

Jeanne sensed his inner turmoil. She pressed his forearm with silent and soulful determination, as on other occasions during their married life. But they were ready to confront the soldiers, even though they had both secretly hoped their house would be passed over, given Jacob's status.

He was a landowner and wealthy merchant now, had been so since the decree five years earlier that had forced Huguenot notaries to either sell their practice or abjure. His organisational skills had served him well in managing his farms and selling their produce of fruit, cattle and cereal. He was one of the first to plant maize, the versatile crop from the New World, in the great fertile plain that surrounded the town. He had also become quite a botanist, and studied water usage and plant requirements for more efficient growth. This resulted in recent yields being constantly higher than average, and his conversion from records of law to record yields had not transpired without some envy.

God had come to try them before; if it pleased Him to try them again then so be it, Jeanne had told him. They would face up to this hurdle in the same way that they had confronted Jacob's professional reconversion, with unwavering resolve without straying from the road of God's love and ultimate reward.

She ushered the children up the stairs to their first-floor rooms. That was the plan.

The doorknocker hammered again.

'King's men, open the door!' hurled a soldier's voice.

Jacob gave the nod to Anette to open up as he joined her in the vestibule where she stood at the front door, speechless and mouse-like.

'This the house of Jacob Delpech?' said the tall, rugged figure that dwarfed her, even though she was standing two steps higher.

'Yes, sir, I am he,' said Jacob stepping into view. 'Whom do I have the pleasure of…'

Lieutenant Ducamp had no time for bourgeois talk. He had a job to do. He held out his billet and read. 'Conforming with the law, Monsieur Jacob Delpech shall give quarter to nine soldiers and will give to these soldiers light, board and lodging.'

In times of conflict soldiers were lodged with the lower classes for a specified number of days.

'You must be mistaken,' said Jacob, feigning not to understand what was happening. 'I am Jacob Delpech de Castanet.'

'Read for yourself, Jacob Delpech de Castanet!' growled the lieutenant holding up the billet in Jacob's face.

Didier Ducamp had seen the same mock incomprehension before in Bearn. It was becoming a bore. Did the bourgeois really think they were dealing with morons? He had to admit though, he had fallen for the comedy the first couple of times. On those occasions he had marched back to his commanding officer to check his information. However, now with experience, not to mention a right rollicking from his commander, he had learnt to disregard any theatricality and get on with the mission at hand.

When he thought about it now, it made him laugh to think that he, who feared neither God nor the devil, had become a better missionary than the Bishop of Bearn.

He pushed his way into the premises. His men followed suit without a thought for the boot scraper, and soon smells of sweat, oil, powder, leather and horse shit filled the largest reception room of the house.

It was always an eye-opener to see how the other half lived. Useless ornaments on carved and embroidered furniture, paintings and tapestries on walls, and books, rows of them all leather bound, always a good sign of prosperity. Oh yes, money has left its mark here. It was a reassuring thought because he and his men could eat a stableful of horses. This, he sensed, would be better than the last billet in Pau which was barren as an old hen. And it had turned out messy too.

The slip of a hand had accidentally popped the proprietor's neck while they were helping him drink a 'restorative' to give him courage to abjure. Of course, the lieutenant had learnt since that you have to be extra careful how you handle pen pushers, soft as young pigeons!

As the eight mercenaries in the pay of the King traipsed into the room, Didier Ducamp turned to his second in command, and gave him a hardly perceptible nod of appreciation. It meant there was no point rushing this one, at least, not while the storehouse was full and their bellies empty.

'Bring us bread, meat, cheese and wine,' said Lieutenant Ducamp.

'Listen here, sir, you really ought to check with the intendant. I am a gentleman…'

'And we are the King's men!' said Ducamp. 'And hungry men with it. Now, do you love and respect your King?'

'I do.'

'Do you respect the law of this land?'

'Yes, sir.'

'Then fetch us our grub and grog, unless you prefer we help ourselves!'

Jacob could but agree to do as was required of him.

'We'll find our quarters ourselves,' said Ducamp.

The next moment the wooden staircase was trembling under the footfall of nine massive men-at-arms. Jeanne was on her way down, with her children in tow, having considered it would be better to keep them with her.

'Gentlemen,' she said boldly and with an empathetic smile. She managed to not let the organic stench of manure and body fluids overpower her nerve. 'We have prepared a large room for you on the second floor where you will be comfortable, I am sure.'

The soldiers laughed out loud and barged past her without a thought for her condition. Indeed it was fortunate she was standing, with her children filed behind her like goslings, on the wide intermediate landing. Otherwise she may well have been flattened against the wall.

'My mother is with baby, sirs, please have some respect!' said a determined little voice. It belonged to Paul, Jeanne's son of seven.

A soldier leered back over the banister with an amused jeer. But he was not staring at the boy. He was looking at his elder sister, Elizabeth. The soldier seemed to be sizing her up, then he looked away in exasperation.

'Bah, flat as a battledore!' he grumbled.

His marching partner behind him then quipped: 'Give it another six months. If it bleeds it breeds, that's what my ol' man used to say.'

By now, Jacob was standing at the foot of the stairs.

'Gentlemen, I protest,' he said firmly. 'Not under my roof will thou speak foul!'

He took his wife's hand and led her down into the vestibule and into the dining-room while the soldiers continued into the first floor corridor.

The bedroom doors upstairs could be heard being rattled, and forced open one by one. This was invariably followed by the clang of metal landing on the floor followed by the squeak of bed springs.

The harassment, though not physical, had shattered Jacob's sense of justice. It harked back to the day when he was told he would have to give up his practice. Then too it had felt that his world was about to cave in. However, as then, he still had his faith, and the love of his wife. She placed a hand on his shoulder as they knelt down to pray.

*

A good thing his uninvited guests missed the scene, busy as they were with their installation upstairs.

Jacob had got to his feet by the time the soldiers reappeared. They were visibly satisfied with the self-attributed quarters and now were ready for food.

They had been marching from Bearn since Friday. Bakers, who had been commissioned to produce bread in abundance, had not been able to provide enough for four thousand extra mouths. And by the time Ducamp had entered the town, albeit early morning, there was not a *quignon* of bread to be found. Was this the way to treat men who risked their lives in war? They had finished their own provisions of dried sausage and were now so ravenous they would put raw flesh between their teeth.

On seeing nothing served, panic, a sense of injustice,

then the fire of wrath, consumed the pit of their bellies where only hunger had previously growled. One soldier grabbed Jacob by the lapels, slammed him against the panelling. The thick-set man brought Jacob's face level with his own, and, in a Germanic accent, he bellowed: 'Food, where's the bloody food! You want me ask your fat wench?'

'Easy, Willheim, man!' said Ducamp with the stamp of authority. 'Remember what happened last time!'

Between gritted teeth the dragoon growled something in German, and let Jacob drop to the floor. A second later Monique, the old cook, thankfully shuffled in with a leg of ham, bread, cheese, a wicker-covered jug of wine and pewter tankards. Ducamp's soldiers lunged for the table with their knives and sat down astride the benches.

'Thank you,' said Jacob, wiping the soldier's saliva from his face.

Didier Ducamp stood tall and stoic, in spite of the scare that reminded him he was responsible for containing these savages, and that he would have to be vigilant at all times. He said to Jacob: 'If you want us out of here, you know what to do. Abjure, man!'

This is the end of this excerpt. MERCHANTS OF VIRTUE is available in print, eBook and audio formats at Amazon on-line stores.

ABOUT THE AUTHOR

Paul C.R. Monk is the author of the Huguenot Chronicles historical fiction trilogy and the Marcel Dassaud books. You can connect with Paul on Twitter at @pcrmonk, on Facebook at www.facebook.com/paulcrmonkauthor and you can send him an email at paulmonk@bloomtree.net should the mood take you.

To receive Paul's newsletter, please go to the subscribe page on his website at www.paulcrmonk.com.

ALSO BY PAUL C.R. MONK

Have you read them?

In the HUGUENOT CHRONICLES Trilogy

MERCHANTS OF VIRTUE (Book 1)

France, 1685. Jeanne is the wife of a once-wealthy merchant, but now she risks losing everything. Louis XIV's soldiers will stop at nothing to forcibly convert the country's Huguenots to Catholicism. The men ransack Jeanne's belongings and threaten her children. If Jeanne can't find a way to evade the soldiers' clutches, her family will face a fate worse than poverty and imprisonment. They may never see each other again…

VOYAGE OF MALICE (Book 2)

Geneva, 1688. Jeanne dreams of her previous life as a wealthy merchant's wife before Louis XIV's soldiers ran her family out of France for refusing to renounce their faith. Jacob hopes his letters make it to Jeanne from the other side of the ocean. As he bides his time as an indentured servant on a Caribbean plantation, tragedy strikes in the form of shipwreck and pirates. If Jeanne and Jacob can't rise above a world that's closing all its doors, then they may never be reunited again...

LAND OF HOPE (Book 3)

A 17th Century family torn apart. A new power on the throne. Will one man reunite with his wife and child, or is he doomed to die in fresh battles? Land of Hope is the conclusion to the riveting Huguenot Chronicles historical fiction trilogy.

Other works

STRANGE METAMORPHOSIS

When a boy faces a life-changing decision, a legendary tree sends him on a magical expedition. He soon has to vie with the bugs he once collected for sport! The journey is fraught with life-threatening dangers, and the more he finds out about himself, the more he undergoes a strange metamorphosis.

"A fable of love and life, of good and evil, of ambition and humility."

Winner of the LITERARY CLASSICS Eloquent Quill Youth Fiction Book Award.

SUBTERRANEAN PERIL

Set in the story-world of Strange Metamorphosis, this action-packed novelette offers a thrilling episode of a boy's fabulous and scary adventure of self-discovery. When 14 year-old Marcel leads his crew out of a dark and disused snake tunnel in search of fresh air, little does he know he is entering the labyrinthic galleries of an ant nest.

Made in the USA
Coppell, TX
03 March 2024